The Maginot Line

The Maginot Line

The Fiction Desk Anthology Series
Volume Three

Edited by Rob Redman

The Fiction Desk

First published in the UK in 2012 by The Fiction Desk Ltd.

ISBN 978-0-9567843-4-6

The Fiction Desk
PO Box 116
Rye
TN31 9DY

Please note that we do not accept postal submissions.
See our website for submissions information.

www.thefictiondesk.com

The Fiction Desk Ltd
Registered in the UK, no 07410083
Registered office: 3rd Floor, 207 Regent Street, London, W1B 3HH

Printed and bound in the UK by Imprint Digital.

Contents

Contents

Introduction

Rob Redman

In the introduction to our first anthology, I wrote briefly about the background to the series, and why I decided to relaunch The Fiction Desk as a publishing house. In *All These Little Worlds*, I wrote a little about the process of putting the anthologies together, why we don't do themed anthologies, and the way themes have a habit of emerging anyway. (There's at least one running theme in this volume too, but this time I'll leave it, or them, for you to discover for yourself.)

This time, I thought I'd write about something really superficial: our covers.

We try to have a broad editorial policy, but it more or less amounts to a focus on traditional narratives with strong characters. To reflect those traditional values, I set certain limitations for our cover images: the designs can only consist of paper and the written word.

The cover of *Various Authors* was in my mind for almost as long as the anthology series itself. I made a couple of tests by hacking away at scrap paper with a fruit knife, before upgrading to a sheet torn from a sketchbook (but still the same fruit knife) for the final version. The handwritten text is a deliberately rambling version of the editorial policy, and specifically talks about our openness to genre, and the limitations of that; I seem to remember there being some reference to elves, although I can't find it on the cover now. The reference was not entirely complimentary.

The figures were drawn on the back of the paper, cut out along three sides and folded to stand up. I think it worked rather well, and it might be my favourite cover to date if not for the rather shouty typesetting of the title (which I've done my best to tidy up in subsequent volumes).

The crumpled sheets of paper on the cover of *All These Little Worlds* are pages torn out of advance copies of *Various Authors*; copies that had been sent out to bookshops but returned to us with their envelopes marked 'closed down' or 'out of business'. Each one therefore represents a different vanished bookshop, and while the title was originally intended to refer to the stories themselves, in retrospect it could equally apply to those lost shops. The chalk was a nice bit of synchronicity given that the anthology ended up containing several stories related to education. (Technically those chalked lines probably aren't 'the written word', making this a small bending of the rules, but we can call them dashes if you like.)

The cover of the present volume is based on the story 'The Maginot Line', which opens the anthology, and from which it takes its name. There's a significance to the kind and order of the leaves, but you'll discover that for yourself when you read Matt's excellent story. This was the first cover for which I allowed myself real tools, rather than kitchen utensils: The Fiction Desk's petty cash stretched to a cutting mat and craft knife.

The background to this cover is a sheet of paper made of elephant poo, which seemed to have the right sort of texture.

Make of that what you will.

Matt hails from Brighton, where he has also edited his own short fiction magazine, Tall Tales & Modern Fables. *I like to believe that editing other people's work helps a writer's own prose, and I offer the following story as evidence.*

The Maginot Line

Matt Plass

Last time it was a wild man in the woods. This time it might be murmurs from the cellar. Or a UFO over Friar's Hill. Or the Chinese.

As always, the phone call from my father begins with a tetchy 'Hello? Hello?' as if I have called him.

'Dad, this is George. You've rung me. On the telephone. Is everything okay?'

For years I lived in the same village as my parents; a two-minute walk from the house where I was raised. After my kids escaped to start their own lives, I sold up and moved into town, a staggering twelve miles away. Now my father bellows at me down the line; increasing the volume to make up for the extra distance between us.

'George, it's your father. Are you listening; can you hear me? George!'

I lay my book flat and take the cordless phone out into the garden. Clear skies, cold air. A triangle of aeroplane lights at forty thousand feet, tiny burning coals cruising far away from here.

'Dad, I can hear you.'

'George. I know it's late but something's not quite right. I thought you ought to know.'

'Are you at home?'

'Of course, it's Wednesday.'

'Are you in the living room?'

'I'm in the kitchen by the vegetable thingy, by the picture window. The woods are behaving very strangely.'

The woods. Three acres separating Holt Cottage from Winterstow Farm, a forgotten swatch of woodland: oak, ash, wild cherry, birch, a huddle of field maple, one extraordinary, ancient willow hazel. Our family's garden beyond the garden. I ask what he means by behaving strangely.

'As in not normal. Sinister. Something's not right, George, and I thought you ought to know. Thanks for calling.'

I sigh and reach for my wellingtons. I'll be out in the damp woods tonight, torch in hand, telling the trees to behave themselves.

I'm in the car on the road I know so well, drifting into dark woods and half remembered conversations with my father. We cut sticks (he called them strods) to help us up the hills. Sundays, we'd walk from Church Farm to Pickham's Mill and back again. And I'd demand a story each way.

'Now, you have to realise,' he'd begin. 'Not a soul in the village would admit to a word of what I'm about to tell you.' Which was, of course, the perfect start.

Those bizarre rural comic strips. *The labourer*, an ugly, heavy man from the valleys with swollen eyes and hands like engine blocks, passing through the village one day between the wars, strong in the arm but weak on common sense, who took a shine to the landlord's daughter at the Royal Oak. She sought respite through the kitchen door and he lumbered after. The well-oiled locals at the bar were already on their feet when they heard the first shrill scream from the pub garden.

'What happened next, son? Hard to say in all that confusion, and there was no moon. It's possible, unlikely mind, but possible the bugger fled down Pannel Lane. Or got away over the fields into Fairlight Wood.'

'This much I know,' Dad would whisper. 'While several people saw the stranger enter the village from the north end, no one ever saw him leave.'

Or the tale of *Jack and Roly*. A disputed piece of land and a furious confrontation between Jack Shine and Roly Summers on the sand bar by Pett Pools. Later, as Roly walked home, there was an accident. Roly drowned.

'And no one,' breathed Dad as we crested Butts Brow. 'No one mentioned the dispute to the investigating constable. But when Jack Shine went up to turn over his new plot, burned into the corn stubble were the words, *Jack the drowner*.'

My headlights pick out a signpost, stark white against the tree line as I take the right fork towards Pett Village. The road narrows.

Since Mum passed, Dad has suffered...how to put this... he's suffered an increasingly uneasy relationship with his environment. The house has turned against him; the woods out back spy on him. Voices whisper in the dark when he's putting out the bins.

I receive an emergency call once a fortnight. Dad's seen something in the garden and he thinks I ought to know. I drive over to Rosemary Lane and we shine a torch into the shed, patrol the dustbins, secure the perimeter. Back in the glow of the kitchen we remind ourselves that foxes are bolder these days. And an old house creaks, especially at night when the heating cuts out and its wooden skeleton cools and contracts.

Then we have a cup of tea and I let him talk about my mother, his wife. By the time I leave, there never were any red eyes in the sky or whispers from the attic.

'Thanks for coming over, son. Mind the road now.'

The canopy thickens as I negotiate Rosemary Lane. I turn into Dad's driveway and keep the unkempt hedges to my left until I reach the house. A crunch of tyres on gravel, then silence except for the tick of the cooling engine. This could be the only house for miles.

There he is, at the window. He's seen the headlights. I hope he recognised what they were.

Dad comes out to meet me in slippers and dressing gown over corduroy trousers, shirt and tie. He is back lit by the strong yellow porch light and for a second I think he's holding out a watchman's lantern. No, it's just an arm raised against the headlights.

'Dad, how are you doing?'

'George? I heard the car, wasn't sure.'

'Thought I'd pop over for a cup of tea, see how you are getting on.'

The house is both warm and clean: two good signs. We go through to the kitchen where the kettle steams. Dad already has a mug on the side. I make myself some tea and complete a quick mental inventory. The cupboards are stocked, sugar in the sugar bowl, bins emptied.

Dad leans against the larder door and takes his mug in both hands. He shaved today, the shirt was clean on.

'Help yourself to biscuits,' he says. 'I just refilled the barrel.'

Telling me to stop snooping. That I'd find no signs of decline here.

'Did you get out today?'

'The leaves by the gate were a nuisance. I had to take the broom up the path.'

Through the sash window I can just make out the low border fence and the trees beyond.

'On the phone you mentioned something about the woods. Everything okay?'

Dad sips his tea.

I close the gap between us with a step. 'You said the woods were behaving strangely.'

Dad clatters his empty mug in the sink. 'I figured it out. All fine now.'

I wait. It works.

Dad says, 'Well, the woods have always...we've not always seen eye to eye.'

Talking to my Dad is like talking to my teenage son, Danny. You have to tweezer information from him like splinters from a palm. Dad and Danny work from an invisible script: I speak, but they respond to different cues.

There are other similarities. At night, I worry. Are Dad and Danny safely in their beds? I fret about their capacity to manage money, their vulnerability to malevolent strangers and their general fecklessness. And there are the phone calls at two a.m. that never bring good news. Both of them so obviously lack the requisite tools for life: Danny yet to acquire them, Dad rapidly discarding them.

'You talk about the woods as if they're people, Dad.'

He says, 'I used to spend a lot of time out back, you remember? Clearing windfalls and cutting back brambles. I'd take Nelson along the path before breakfast for his morning regulars. It was a good place for me. You could walk for an hour and meet no one.'

More childhood memories, this time of the woods: running ahead to lay an ambush, only to be betrayed by bloody Nelson the dog. Naming the matrix of woodland footpaths: the Orient Express, the London to Brighton, the Yellow Brick Road. And spanning the border of our garden, a row of trees that Dad called the Maginot Line.

Our conversations: some organic and some, I realised later, contrived, Kiplingesque. On those walks I learned that to be brave you must first be afraid; that I should respect others, but never too much. I learned the rewards of perseverance, the benefits of hard work. And other more esoteric rules: Don't trust a man with beavery teeth. Set aside three days' salary when buying shoes. Don't go out with wet hair. Always stand a drink for the barman when it's your round. Don't mix grape and grain. Give people what they need not what they want. Don't swim within an hour of eating lunch or you will drown.

I join Dad at the window and we study our reflections, our thoughts projected into the woods beyond the glass.

I tell him it's a special place for all of us. 'Even Danny enjoys being there and he hates everything.'

'This morning I went out back to fetch the big brush from the shed. Now, on my way to the shed I didn't notice anything. But on my way back... .' With one finger, Dad draws a thick horizontal worm in the condensation. 'I've been staring at that treeline for over fifty years. I know it like my tongue knows my teeth.'

Dad hasn't had his own teeth since the Berlin Wall came down.

'I know those trees like the keys on a piano,' he says. 'And this morning there was something different, something not right. They were closer, bunched. The fat oak was leaning in to that raggedy ash where you used to have your swing. The birches were huddled by the gate. It should have been tree, tree, tree, space, tree, space, tree. But it was tree, tree, big space, tree, tree, tree.'

My face betrays me. Dad says, 'I don't care how unlikely you think it is. Maybe things like that don't happen in the city but it happened here.'

I peer through the glass but there's only darkness beyond. 'Trees shift over time, Dad. Hard to notice if you are looking at them every day.'

This cuts no ice. I accept the inevitable. 'Shall we take a look, together?'

'You wouldn't be able to see the difference.'

That's enough. 'I'm not exactly a stranger here. I grew up in that garden.'

'You won't see the difference, George, because they are back in line now. They had their little union meet and went back to work.'

'Grab your coat, Dad.'

It's still clear outside, still cold. We latch the kitchen door and skirt the vegetable plot towards the far end of the garden. Dad walks ahead, swinging his car torch like an air raid searchlight. At the top of its arc, the beam picks out the Maginot Line: the oak, the ash, the birches, the gate; and suddenly we have run out of path. We pull up abruptly at the foot of the garden, two generals inspecting a parade.

'This is how I remember them,' I say.

'Back to normal, now.'

We stand in silence for a minute. But it's only silent while your ears adjust to the sounds of the night. The longer we stand there, the more I hear: an owl, a furtive scraping in the hedgerow to my left, the trees, even in these light winds, softly swaying and moaning, and...moving?

'Dad, what did you mean when you said the trees had finished their little union meeting?'

'I won't have the tail wag the dog. I won't. A peace offering every now and then. But it can't become a habit.'

'You made a peace offering to the trees?'

'Don't think I didn't hear their muttering, George. Huh! Look, I'm not without sympathy. I get it...I used to be out here every day. It was me cutting back the brambles and trimming the hedges. We're not on the rambler's route, the council doesn't care. But I can't do all that now, I just can't. It's young man's work.'

'And you think the woods resent you for it?'

'That's what all this nonsense was about. I saw them, conspiring in their little huddles. That oak is the bloody shop steward. Anyway, I got the message and took the saw out there to trim back some of the hedge by the path. Nearly killed me just lifting the bloody saw but I did it.'

Cutting back the hedgerow: Dad's peace offering.

'The thing is George, it seems to have quietened them. But for how long? I just can't work out there like I used to. What am I going to do?'

Suddenly I understand. We walk back up the path to the house. I tell Dad what an amazing job he did all these years, how the woods owe everything to him and how grateful I am to have had such a marvellous playground. I remind him how Mum often walked the long way home to bring her through the woods. I tell him he won't be forgotten around here but I stop short of saying that the trees will miss him, although I know that's what he wants to hear.

I promise to come over regularly and clear the paths, keep the hedges in line. We laugh at my chances of getting Danny to help. Together, we drink another cup of tea.

Later, sat in my warm modern car, I watch Dad wave goodbye from the doorway and wonder what it will be like when my life is so small I can hold it in the palm of one hand.

As I ease out into Rosemary Lane night fills the car and I make a decision. I shall place a memorial here after he's gone, a bench in the woods with a copper plaque engraved with his name and dates.

I ask myself if it's ever okay to erect a memorial bench for someone who's still alive. Before he goes, I'd like Dad to see his bench planted out there in the woods, surrounded by the oaks and the ash; his permanent seat at the table.

Mandy Taggart usually writes flash fiction, and other pieces a little shorter than the stories we normally publish. I've been hoping for a while that she'd send us something longer, and 'The Man of the House' was certainly worth the wait.

The Man of the House

Mandy Taggart

Jack sits in his armchair and looks around the living room, in the house that has been his place for as long as he can remember. He sits and listens to Louise telling the woman with the soft voice that she wants Jack to go away.

He's been expecting this for a while, but pretending to himself that it would never really happen. Most of the time, these days, Jack tries to stay unnoticed in his corner, for fear of causing any more distress. He used to try to attract Louise's attention, but he's decided to give that up, because it's often worse than not being noticed at all. It makes her look at him with fear and confusion in her eyes. He racks his brains to remember what it was that he did or said that upset her; but it's gone, all gone.

And he never dares to call to the children any more. He hates the thought of upsetting them, but can't seem to avoid it. One night last week, he woke in his armchair, heard little Ryan crying upstairs and tried to start going up to him, even though it was hard for him to get out of the chair. He had to go, because he knew it was the danger that was making Ryan cry, and he needed to save him. Jack had fallen asleep, and the danger had got upstairs. You can't leave a four-year-old alone with the danger. It might eat him.

He'd got himself half way up the stairs, and the poor little boy was standing at the top, screaming down at him. The danger must have frightened him out of his bed. Jack had his arms held wide, trying to get there in time to stop Ryan from falling, but he was slow, so slow. Then came Louise, barging past him and she snatched up the child, wheeled round with a wild face staring down at Jack as if *he* was the one who had made Ryan cry. He reached out to them, tried to explain about the danger, but it all came out wrong. It all came out just like noises, and then Louise screamed as well, and woke Maisie. She carried Ryan away, still bellowing into her shoulder, went and lifted Maisie out of the cot and the three of them all slept together in Louise's bedroom that night. Jack didn't dare to go near them, so he lay down on the landing floor to protect them, all night curled in a ball outside the closed door. The danger didn't try again that night, just to make him feel foolish.

Even the dog doesn't like him any more: Champion, his old friend. He tries to whistle to him, but the dog growls and he remembers that it's a mistake. Champion was killed years ago on the road out there, and this is just another dog who looks like him. Jack forgets his name.

And all the time Louise rushes around the house, trying to bring up her children without a husband. At first Jack was annoyed with her – the young people won't stick with a marriage these days, for better or worse – but, from what he's heard her saying on the telephone since then, that Darren of hers was no good anyway. Jack would give him a piece of his mind if he ever dared to show his face in this house. Teach him a man's responsibilities.

Jack takes his own responsibilities very seriously. You can't always see the danger, but it's there all the same. Last night, the grill came on all by itself and filled the kitchen with smoke, nearly smothered them all in their beds, and Jack knows that Louise thinks it was him but it wasn't. Really, it wasn't. He pushed himself to the limit last night, got himself out of the chair and across the black billowing kitchen, managed to shift the catch on the door to the utility room and let in good old Champion; no, not Champion, the other dog. And Champion barked and howled the place down, standing his ground in the kitchen with the hackles raised and the lips tunnelling up over the teeth, inching towards Jack and then backing off again. Woke them all up and everybody was safe, but Louise thinks it was Jack who put the grill on, and it wasn't. It was the danger.

The lights turning off, and that face in the TV: those things aren't Jack, either. He can't understand why Louise is telling the soft-voiced woman that he's been doing that as well. He was sitting right across the room from her, the last time the lights went out. The children were both asleep upstairs and Jack sat in the dark, listening to Louise sobbing and pleading in the armchair opposite him, straining his ears to be sure that the danger wasn't hurting her. It broke his heart. After a while he tried to call out to Louise, calm her down, tell her that at least she knew that hadn't been him. But it all came out wrong, just the noises again, and then everything got worse.

He remembers May, his wife, and his own marriage. Their three girls running around this house, hanging their stockings up on the fireplace. Not this fireplace, the old one, made of brick. Jack can conjure this memory until he can almost hear the flapping of skirts, their laughter precious like glass. He knows that he'd remember the names of all the girls, if only his mind wasn't all taken up with responsibilities. It was different in those days. The danger hardly ever showed itself, and could be dispatched for months by a steady mind and one firm look over the shoulder of a crying child. But Jack isn't sure: his memory comes and goes. Maybe, back then, there was no danger at all. Or maybe it was a different sort of danger.

He hopes that he was a good man for May. Worked hard, taught all the girls to ride their bicycles, helped them with their homework. Helped May, too, through the bad times, when she cried and screamed that the children had tied her to the house, that her mind was like an empty space, that she could never get out the door. He held her tight, held her back sometimes. Promised that he would stay with her. That's what the young people don't understand any more, that a promise must never be broken. Even when there's no way of telling, when you're making that promise, what it really means.

When the girls grew up and moved away, he wished them well. Wept, but understood, when they never came back. Looked over at May, sitting opposite him by the fire, and she smiled into his eyes. But then May died, and Champion was killed, and the danger slid into all the empty spaces. For a long time, it was just the two of them here. He got the full measure of the danger, in those years. He worries that it may already have had the full measure of him.

But then came Louise and the children, Ryan and Maisie, on his doorstep in desperation. Needing to come here and live with him. He found that he couldn't tell them about the danger, and this worries him: but having their company and noise in the house makes him feel alive again. Sometimes Jack sees Louise as a daughter, here with his grandchildren, and sometimes he can't remember who they all are. But Louise needs him, all right, whoever she is. A responsible man in the house, while she's crying over that Darren night after night.

At night, while they're sleeping, he drags himself up, silent as he can, in through the bedroom doors and stands guard over them, each in turn, until the morning. For a few weeks it was like the old days. His presence alone, his strength and his gaze, seemed to be enough. Otherwise, the danger would surely have got them already, with him too slow now to hold it back.

But recently it's been getting worse; Jack can feel it. The danger is gathering strength, has found more space somewhere. Jack thinks that the space is in the crying, the longing for Darren that Louise won't let go of. This is a time when Jack must be firm in his place, learn new ways to fight the danger. But Louise is trying to get him out of the house.

'Perhaps he'll cause a scene,' she is whispering to the soft-voiced woman. 'He thinks of this as his home. He won't want to leave. But we can't go on like this. It's upsetting the children.'

'Then I'll explain things to him gently,' says the soft voice. 'Poor soul. He's just confused. I'm sure he doesn't mean to cause trouble, but he does, doesn't he? Like last week, on the stairs. I'm sure that, when he was himself, he wouldn't have wanted that at all.'

This can't happen. Jack will not be turned out. He has to protect Louise and the children from the danger. Lord knows he'd prefer to rest in his old age. Sometimes he feels as if he just sat down in his chair one day, after May died, and woke up and years had gone by and he couldn't just rise out of the chair and move about like he used to. Getting out of the chair is a struggle, out of the room still harder, and out of the house is impossible. House bound, he is. But not a liability, no matter what Louise says. He's the man of the house.

The talking has stopped now, and the curtain between the living room and kitchen moves aside for the soft-voiced woman to come in. Jack thinks of closing his eyes and pretending to sleep, but that would be weakness. He needs to keep his wits about him.

The soft-voiced woman comes in and sits down in the chair opposite him. She frowns slightly as she does so, but her face is open and friendly. He expected a uniform, but she's in brightly coloured clothes, scarves and silver bangles, hair a cheerful red like dark cherries. It does him good to look at her. And she talks to Jack, this woman. Looks properly at him like nobody has looked at him in years. Listens to him, really listens, and he finds himself telling her everything. She seems to understand, even when the words come out wrong.

When he's finished explaining, he looks at her, waiting. The woman frowns again.

'I understand,' she says, and goes out. He hears her sit down at the kitchen table, imagines her taking Louise's hand.

'I've had a good look, my darling, and you're absolutely right. In this house is the spirit of an elderly man, the one you've been seeing. He lived here before, and never moved on.'

Hearing the words said aloud sends the cold echo of a pulse through Jack.

'I can make him leave, if you want,' she says, 'but I wouldn't recommend it. He's been protecting you from the other one, you see. And *that* one is tied to this house. It can never leave.'

Jack leans back in his chair and continues his watch. The man of the house, protecting Louise and the children until they leave him. Which they surely will, as soon as they can. And after that, he'll stay here, with the danger. He promised.

Jack raises his eyebrows at the danger, looks her in the eyes. And from the armchair opposite, the woman of the house stares back at him with half a dead smile.

Justin is a former journalist living in West Virginia, where he teaches undergraduate writing. On the evidence of his own work, I'd say his students are in safe hands.

Automatic Pilot

Justin D. Anderson

Carl knew his wife Martha had been fired when he saw her car already parked in the driveway. She usually got home from work an hour after he did. He pulled his pickup in beside her car and stopped and looked at the wooden beads she had dangling from the rearview. The beads had spiritual powers, Martha believed. He didn't believe it. She'd bought them at the grocery store in a checkout line. He sat in the idling truck for a few moments and looked at the beads, his hands draped over the top of the steering wheel. He dropped his head and shook it slow and turned off the engine.

He got out of the truck and walked up to the little front patio of the house and sat down on the concrete. He looked up and down the street. All the old oaks standing in the grass strips along the curbs and in some of the neighbours' yards had succumbed to some kind of blight. It was summer and there wasn't a leaf on any of them. The street and yards were littered with dead branches.

The Hudsons across the street weren't home yet. In their front yard, a huge branch from one of the oaks there had fallen and caved in the roof above their living room. The branch rested on the bottom sill of the bay window. Truss boards jutted around the branch like horrible teeth. Through that window, Carl sometimes watched Tom and Nancy Hudson sitting in the evenings watching television with their socked feet up on the coffee table. The room was always softly lit by the little lamp on the table next to the sofa. Sometimes one of the Hudsons would say something to the other, and the other would laugh. Sometimes Nancy would give Tom a light slap on the arm. Or sometimes one of them would leave the room briefly and then hurry back to the sofa to resume this togetherness. They didn't have children and they seemed content with each other. Carl would watch from his own living room while Martha was upstairs, giving their little daughter Lucy a bath. Watching the Hudsons made Carl wonder how he and Martha would be if they didn't have Lucy. It horrified him to imagine it.

Carl couldn't help but grin a little looking over at the damage. He kept thinking of the Hudsons coming home and how without any alarm or dismay, they would get out of their car, climb up on that branch, and walk it like they were crossing a creek down into their living room. And how they would sit together as usual among those ruins. They were like that, the Hudsons. They were young. It made Carl feel good thinking of how they were still so young and it was just the two of them. Carl slapped his knees and went inside.

Martha had already picked up Lucy from day care and Carl found them at the kitchen table. Lucy gripped a crayon and drew on a big white sheet of paper. Martha looked up at Carl. She smiled sadly and then looked back down at what Lucy was drawing.

'That's beautiful, honey,' she said. 'Make Mommy something pretty. She needs it.'

'It happened?' Carl said.

Martha kept watching Lucy.

'Yes,' she said. 'Mommy got let go today, didn't she honey?'

'Lay-go,' Lucy said.

'Christ,' Carl said. 'I'm sorry, honey.'

He walked into the kitchen and sat down at the table on the other side of Lucy and rubbed her hair. He went to touch Martha's hand resting on the table, but she pulled it back and put it under the table with her other hand.

'What did they say?' Carl said.

Martha said something low to Lucy.

'Martha,' Carl said. 'Was it about the money?'

'They didn't say anything about why,' Martha said.

'That doesn't make sense.'

Martha shrugged and kept her hands under the table.

'Who fires someone without telling them why?' Carl said.

'Well, that's what happened,' Martha said.

Carl stood up and walked over to the sink full of dirty dishes and pots from dinner the night before. He put his hands on the sides of the sink and stared down at the mess. Then he looked up through the window over the sink, and could see the three dead oaks in the backyard; one of them stood close to the house. Dead branches were all over the yard.

'We should cut those down,' Carl said.

'What?'

'Those oaks out back. A branch smashed in the Hudsons' living room.'

'I saw that,' Martha said. She watched Lucy, who was turning the big pad of paper to a new page. 'Draw Mommy a farm. Farms are nice.'

Carl started to tell her about how he'd imagined the Hudsons coming home, but he stopped. He turned on the water in the sink and started to wash the dishes.

'I'll get those dishes,' Martha said.

'You just need to take it easy.'

'Why?'

'Because you got shit-canned,' he said. 'That'd be a hard thing to take.'

Martha giggled and brought her hands up on the table.

'What's funny?' Carl said.

'Mommy knew it was going to happen,' she said to Lucy. 'Didn't she? Mommy and Daddy both knew.'

'I didn't know,' Carl said. He wiggled his fingers under the water.

'Come on, Carl. Let's not kid ourselves. Dog eat dog, you know?'

'I didn't think they would. They had no proof of anything. Besides, it was a lie. Right?'

'We knew it was coming.'

'*I* didn't, I said.'

'Daddy knew, didn't he?' Martha said.

'Daddy knew,' Lucy said. She looked at her father and made a funny face.

Carl looked back at the sink. He poured some blue dish soap out on a sponge and worked up a lather.

'What are we going to do?' he said and began scrubbing off plates.

'I guess I'll have to look for another job.'

'You guess?'

'What do you want me to say, Carl?'

'I don't know.' He kept washing the plates and rinsing them, slipping them in the white drain rack on a towel next to the sink.

'We'll be okay for a while,' Carl said. 'But not long.'

'Daddy thinks Mommy's stupid,' Martha said.

'I don't think you're stupid,' Carl said. 'I want to talk about how this happened.'

'I told you. No real reason given.'

'There had to be.'

'She just said it wasn't working out.'

'That's vague enough.' Carl started on a pot. 'Why don't you get the food out of pots before you put them in the sink?'

'That's a lovely farm,' Martha said. Carl pulled the pot out by its handle and swept the food with his fingers into the garbage can under the sink.

'We'll get fruit flies, Martha,' he said. 'They're hard to get rid of. There'll be a cloud of them in here.'

Martha didn't say anything.

'Martha. Did you hear me?'

'Fruit flies,' she said. 'I heard you.'

Carl finished the pot and stacked it in the drying rack. He looked out the window.

'Those goddamned trees,' he said. 'What the hell happened to them?'

'I saw Mr. Brubaker at the gas station the other day and he told me it was some kind of a fungus,' Martha said.

'What does he know?'

'He even had a name for it,' she said. 'Like rammera or something.'

'They're just old. Those trees are probably hundreds of years old.'

Carl scrubbed hamburger grit and grease from a frying pan.

'Draw Mommy a tree now,' Martha said. Lucy flipped to a new sheet in the pad.

Carl rinsed out the pan and leaned it in the drain rack. He turned off the water and wiped his hands with a dishtowel. Then he sat down at the table. He went for Martha's hand again, but she pulled away. Carl leaned back in his chair.

'We have to talk about this, honey,' he said.

'Mommy doesn't want to talk about it.'

'Why don't you talk to me for a while,' Carl said. 'What do you think was the reason?'

Lucy looked up from the paper at Carl and smiled. Carl didn't mean to, but he glared at Lucy and her smile withered and she went back to drawing. Martha picked up a brown crayon and started to draw a tree trunk on the opposite page.

'Martha, you've got some idea about why.'

She kept drawing the tree. 'I did this to myself,' she said.

'Shit.'

'No. I hated that place. I had a hard time getting out of bed in the morning to go to work I hated it so much.'

'I know you did.'

'Don't you think that showed at work? That attitude?'

Carl shrugged. 'I hate my job, too, but I still have it.'

'I guess I can't hide it like you.'

Carl folded his hands on the table. 'I'm sure it wasn't you.'

Martha finished her tree and picked up a yellow crayon and drew a circle, then filled it in.

'Right?' Carl said.

'Maybe it's something *about* me,' she said. 'Something that makes people not like me.' She used a black crayon to draw birds in the sky around the tree and the sun. Lucy on the page opposite wore down a crayon. Then she grabbed another and continued drawing.

'No.'

'Maybe it is,' she said.

'It's the other people, honey. It's them.'

'But what if it's me?'

'It's not. You worked with a bunch of back-stabbing idiots. You said so yourself.'

Now Martha drew a green hill under the tree and another one off to the side. She put a small house with two windows on top of it in red. Carl looked at this drawing and was disappointed. The scene was so typical.

'You work hard and they don't and you were making them look bad,' Carl said. 'So they made up a story about you. A lie.'

Martha shrugged.

'And your boss is lazy. You've said so. It was easier to fire you than defend you.'

'I told her it was a lie,' Martha said, dropping the crayon.

'I know you did.'

'I told her that.'

'I know. It's just like I said, honey. It wouldn't have mattered what you said.'

Carl reached again for his wife's hand and she drew it away. Lucy watched this, then went back to drawing.

'Stop it, Carl,' she said.

'What's wrong with you?' he said.

She looked down at her lap. 'Nothing.'

'Are you telling the truth about the money?'

'Yes.'

'Then what is it?'

'Nothing.'

'Martha.'

'Okay. It was just once. And it was only a few dollars. You were laid off and I needed something. It wasn't a big deal.'

'Jesus, Martha,' he said and shook his head. 'I can't believe this.'

'I'm sorry for lying to you. Everyone did it. It wasn't a big deal. I meant to replace it. It was only a few dollars.'

'Oh, the hell with you, Martha. You've ruined us.'

'I didn't,' she said.

'We're done.'

'We're not. I'll find something else.'

'How?' He raised his hands. 'No one's going to hire you.'

Martha reached toward Carl, but he stood up and paced around the kitchen. Lucy watched them.

'Have you told your mother about getting fired?' he said.

'No.'

'Good. You'd just have to lie to her, too.'

Carl went out the sliding doors to the back yard. He lit a cigarette and walked around and pushed on the trees to see how weak they were. The trees didn't move. He walked around in the grass, running his hand along the top of the chain-linked fence, and smoked.

Martha had made Lucy some dinner while he was outside. They were at the table when he came back in. The girl picked up little meatballs with her fingers and ate them. Carl stood and watched.

'Do you want me to make you something?' Martha said.

'No,' Carl said. 'Who could eat?'

'It's not that serious,' she said. 'They can't give specifics in references, anyway.'

'Christ, I don't even care about that,' he said.

'Then what?'

'All this time,' Carl said. 'All this time you're coming home crying, saying how unfair you were being treated, how everyone was lying about you, trying to push you out, and here's me — dipshit, oblivious me — telling you it's all going to be okay, supporting you, trying to be a good husband,' he said.

'You are a good husband.'

Carl shrugged.

'I try to be,' he said. 'You'd probably make a good wife, too. But you're a liar.'

'Carl, don't. How many times can I apologise before you forgive me about this?'

'I don't care how many times. It'd probably be better if you just said nothing.'

'Carl. We'll get through this.'

'This what?'

'Carl.'

He sat down at the table. It seemed like a long time that the two of them sat and watched Lucy eat her dinner. The girl looked at them and eventually smiled. They smiled back at her. Martha patted the girl's hand. Carl smoothed over her hair, like he always did. The girl asked to take a bath.

'Not tonight,' he said.

'It's okay. I'll give her one, honey.'

'Not tonight. You just relax. You probably need to recover from all of this stress, right? I'm sure the weight of it is unbearable for you.'

'Stop.'

'I mean, I don't know how you can stand it. I don't know how you can stand being so helpless. So put-upon.'

'Stop.'

Carl nodded. He stood up and got a washcloth from a drawer by the sink. He turned on the hot water and waited and then saturated the cloth and wrung it. Martha got up and went down the hall to their bedroom and shut the door. Carl started wiping Lucy's palms. Then her face and neck. He worked on the remnants of the dinner, but they didn't seem to be coming off. He started to scrub. He felt Lucy struggling, trying to pull her face away from the coarseness. But he couldn't stop. Like he was on automatic pilot. He went back to her hands and scrubbed the backs. Then he scrubbed the girl's face again until she whimpered. Then she started to cry. He kept seeing more and more filth on her face. He wanted to make sure he got everything off. Her skin reddened. He knew he was hurting her. He was not a bad person. Everything about this registered with him in a sincere and sentimental way. Like it would anyone else. He felt such a strong tenderness for his daughter. He loved her so much. But he couldn't stop.

Journalist Benjamin Johncock is a familiar name to many in the UK literary scene, making it something of a surprise that this is his first published work of fiction. Remember, you saw him here first! (Even if you think you saw him somewhere else before this.)

The Rocket Man

Benjamin Johncock

Molly sat alone in the kitchen, listening to her father crying upstairs. A minute earlier, the clock that she'd been given at school six months before had begun to count down, and her parents had started to shout at each other. The clock was red and had eight numbers. Now, instead of pointing to eight, the solitary hand indicated seven: seven minutes. Molly stood up, pushing the legs of the chair across the stone floor. She snatched the clock from the table and ran out of the kitchen, through the back door and into the garden.

The house was built of brick, a rare sight now, especially in Montana. It had four stories and a basement that Molly was never allowed into. Her father was a great architect. He'd won prizes. Molly liked to imagine him labouring for years on the design and build, filling his mind with late-night visions of its completion, drawing inspiration from a lifetime of work. 'You blend the old with the new,' he had once told her. 'You welcome the future, without forgetting the past.' The house, large, rural, modern, had seven bedrooms, three washrooms and two preparation rooms (that her father insisted on still calling kitchens, although Molly had noticed that her mother had stopped using this old name six months ago, around the same time as everyone heard the News. All anyone ever talked about from then on was the News. It was as though nothing else mattered).

Outside, the summer air was hot. Molly felt it hit her face as she ran into the garden, gripping the clock in her hand, heading for the woodland at its far end. Crossing into the shade of the trees, Molly's ears readjusted, picking up the clicks and rustles of the undergrowth. The ground sprung and mulched under her bare feet, sending loamy wafts into her nostrils. Invisible birds sung from the branches: the red-naped sapsucker, a plumbeous vireo, the western meadowlark; perhaps a starling. Molly felt peaceful. She looked for her tree. The gnarled yellow buckeye was not hard to find, with a ladder leaning against its trunk. She put her hands on the struts and began to climb, up to a wooden tree house that overlooked the garden. The clock, still tightly gripped in her hand, said five.

A few nights before, Molly was in the kitchen watching the television with her mother and father. The screen was stuck to the refrigerator and a man on it was talking about the News. He asked a psychologist to explain what it would feel like when it happened. Molly didn't understand the answer. After the man had thanked his guest, Molly asked her parents what it was going to feel like after it happened. Her mother shouted at her to 'shut up,' and 'just shut up Molly,' and 'for fuck's sake,' then made a loud noise to no one, like the time she banged her head on the cupboard door. She ripped the television off the refrigerator and threw it across the room. Then she left the house and didn't return until the next day.

Molly stood up in the tree house and turned around. A trapdoor was tied next to the opening, held back by a piece of rope wound around a metal grip on the wall. Molly's father had built the tree house for her sixth birthday. She paused, remembering all the hard work it had taken. It had been the best two weeks of her life. Every morning, he had woken her at six o'clock so they could make the most of the day. It was hot work. They joked and laughed together. His roar and her giggle. Molly's mother would sometimes come down with drinks, or with calls from clients that he always refused to take, even when they were having a break. The woods bristled with the activity of the local wildlife. Molly found an anthill and a bee's nest, all within her new neighbourhood.

'I'd better get rid of them,' her daddy said.

'No, Daddy!' Molly said. 'They are my new neighbours. I am going to invite them round for tea.'

She unwound the rope and lowered the door. It shut tight with a precision that her father had marvelled over when they had finished building it.

'Look at that, Molly,' he had said, opening and closing it. 'Look at that.'

Molly pushed the bolt across the door, locking it from within, and glanced up to the wooden planks above her head. Above them was her special place. It was the safest place she knew. She'd designed it, with her father's help. It was invisible to anyone who didn't know it was there. And the only way you could get in was from the roof. She looked at the clock. There wasn't much time.

It was a school day, but there had been no school for six months. Lessons had been suspended so that the children could spend as much time as possible with their parents. Molly remembered her last lesson with stark clarity. It was the lesson in which the children learned about the News. That morning, Molly was late because of the snow. She crept into her classroom and sat down. Her desk registered her arrival as Mrs Bainburgh walked towards her.

'Molly,' she said, as Molly pulled off her gloves and removed her hat. 'You don't need to get your screen out. Today, I need to talk to you all about something very important.'

Mrs Bainburgh walked back to the front of the room. Molly frowned, took off her coat and listened. Mrs Bainburgh stood before the class and pulled her finger through the air, drawing an imperfect circle in chalk white that hung in front of her.

'This is the sun,' she said. 'It is dying.'

Molly pushed the clock into her pocket and climbed out of the window, pulling her body up with handgrips fixed onto the outside of the tree house. Once she was halfway out, she was able to put her feet on the edge of the window and climb. When she reached the top, she got down on her hands and knees and scrabbled around in the leaves until her fingers felt a circle cut into the wood. Using the palm of her hand, she pushed each of the four compass points carved into it in turn. The circle swung open to reveal a slide. She dropped in, gliding down to a small room below. She sat up. The sheets of light that her daddy had attached to the walls came on and illuminated the space with the murky glow of a fish tank. Scattered across the floor were toys, cushions and blankets. Molly took the clock from her pocket and placed it on the floor. It now said three. Molly felt bad. She shouldn't have run off. Her mummy would be cross. She'd told Molly not to leave the house Under Any Circumstances, as Today Was The Day. Her daddy would know where to find her though. It would be the first place he'd look. He was probably running across the garden to get her right now, before the countdown reached zero. He'd carry her back to the house, her arms wrapped around his neck, and they'd head down together into the Harbour that had been made for them beneath the house.

Everyone in Molly's class had been given a clock. It was made of plastic that reflected her face when she held it up close. Molly had never seen a real clock before, one that she could hold in her hand. It had come in a clear plastic box, with *United States Government* written on the underside.

'Why has it only got eight numbers on it?' Sarah Stewart-Smith said.

'It's a special type of clock,' Mrs Bainburgh said. 'It's a countdown clock.'

It was May and it was cold and the snow fell hard against the plastic windows of the classroom, melting as it touched them. It had been snowing for the last six weeks.

'The United States Government feels that it is important for every child over the age of five to receive teaching on the news that we have recently received from the NASA,' Mrs Bainburgh said. She spoke as if she were teaching mathematics or particle physics. Matter-of-fact. Keep it calm. That's what they'd been told to do; that was the slogan, but inside she felt mushroom clouds sprouting in the caverns of her heart as she watched the little faces avoid her eye. She thought back to when the news was made public. The words still haunted her: the NASA have discovered disturbing irregularities in the solar activity of the sun. The news was simple, but devastating: that, on August seventeenth (exact time of day: unknown) the sun, our G-type main sequence star, the solar of our system, that near-perfect sphere that had burnt since before humanity existed, Hyperion, Helios, Apollo himself,

43

would cease its nuclear fusion of hydrogen to helium. Production would stop. The shop would shut. The star would die. She'd been chopping onions at the time, for a soup. Vegetable. Or was it chicken noodle? When recalling this moment over the days and weeks that followed, the only thing she could remember (apart from the onions) was finding herself sitting on the floor of her kitchen, back against the cupboards, shaking.

'Which of you can tell me how long it takes the light from the sun to reach the Earth?' she said.

Molly glanced around at her classmates. They all were looking down at their desks, at their screens, avoiding the eye of their teacher. Molly touched the front of her desk, which illuminated.

'Molly, yes?' Mrs Bainburgh said.

'Eight minutes,' Molly said.

'Eight minutes! Yes. Thank you, Molly. Eight minutes. It takes eight minutes for the light of the sun to reach us here on Earth.'

She walked over to Sarah Stewart-Smith's desk and picked up her clock.

'Eight minutes. As you know, at some point on August seventeenth the sun will go out. The NASA have astronauts in orbit around Venus who are monitoring the sun very closely. They will let us know when it happens. Once we hear from them, we will only have eight minutes of sunlight left. These clocks are for you. They are not for your parents or your brothers or your uncles. They have their own way. For you.'

She put the clock back down on Sarah Stewart-Smith's desk.

'They will help you keep track, when the time comes.'

Inside the tree house, Molly pulled a large box out of the cupboard. It was black and had almost no mass. You could store heavy things inside it without affecting its overall weight.

Molly used it to hide the objects she cared about the most. She placed it on the crimson rug that covered the floor and sat back down, crossing her legs. She touched the top of the box with her fingers and the lid slid open. It was dark inside. She reached in and took out the first thing that her hand fell on. It was a white stone the size of her fist, an almost-perfect sphere. Her daddy had found it in the woods on the day that she was born. 'It was just there, waiting for me,' he had said. 'Like you.' Molly held the stone in her hand, feeling its weight pull against the tendons in her arm. She felt comforted by the tension, the balance of forces, the rules that governed the world. She put it on the floor next to her and reached back inside. She pulled out an owl's feather, tawny, long-extinct, then a paper book that smelt of wood. She ran her thumb against its edge. It started to disintegrate; the fug of old ink crept into the back of her nostrils making her nose fizz and her eyes water. Molly's hand returned to the box, pushing through a stratigraphy of chattels and ephemera until her fingers wrapped themselves around a cardboard packet. It was red and white and ragged, but a cellophane wrapper had helped to preserve it longer than its manufacturer could have ever foreseen. Molly pushed the cardboard lid open with her thumb and took out one of two remaining smokes. She held it carefully between her finger and thumb as she searched her box for the matches. There were only a handful left. She placed the smoke between her lips and struck the match across the side of the matchbox. It flamed as she drew it up to her face.

Molly's great-grandma had been sent to sleep on the eve of her hundred and fiftieth birthday, like everyone who reached her age. In her Final Document, she'd left Molly a worthless old machine; at least, that's how the lawyer had described it.

'Plastic,' he had said, regarding the object in his hand before handing it to Molly. 'Well I never.' Idiot, Molly thought, clamping her teeth together to stop herself from crying. It's white polycarbonate. Tough as old boots, her great-grandma used to say, who cherished it above all of her other things, as Molly did now. She missed her great-grandma so much. Deep in the box, her hand finally found it. Molly pulled it out. It was about the same size as her box of smokes. The back was silver, corroded with rust and warped towards the bottom. She set it down and picked up a bundle of thin white cord. She pushed her fingers into the twisted ball, pulling it apart like a cat's cradle, holding the tension. She glanced at the clock on the floor. The clock said one.

Molly untangled the cord and pushed the two white rosebuds that were attached to it into her ears. At the other end was an oxidised metallic pin that she pushed into a small hole set into the top of the object. On the front, a screen lit up, casting a blue hue around the room. The machine was filled with short, classical compositions that her great-grandma had put on it years ago. She found one of her favourites, called ROCKET MAN. The familiar piano filled her ears. It was a story about an astronaut back in the old days of space, long ago, when man was leaving the Earth for the first time. Molly felt sorry for him. He missed his family so much when he was away. He was lonely. She imaged him slowly spinning towards the moon in his tin can spacecraft, the blackness of space visible out of a small window, the blue Earth shrinking behind him.

In the kitchen of the house, John Harrison stood, out of breath, staring at his wife. His gut heaved in and out like a mid-Atlantic swell.

'She's nowhere in the house,' he said.

'Oh my God,' she said. 'Oh my God. How long? How long?'

He looked at the time.

'One minute!'

'She was right here! Oh God, John, where is she?'

Molly shut her eyes as she listened to the story. She smiled. At home, the astronaut was a daddy. She made up pictures about it in her mind. He had a boy and a girl. The girl was the youngest. She had red hair, tied in pigtails. Daddy, don't go! she would say. I'll be home soon enough pumpkin, he would say. That was his special name for her. She would jump into his arms and he would hold her tight. Then he would kiss her mummy. Please be careful, she'd say. Who's the best pilot y'ever saw? he'd say, and she'd smile, despite her fears.

John Harrison felt a coolness on his arm. He looked up. The back door was ajar.

'Oh, god, Isabelle, she's outside; she went outside!'

'Oh, no, no no no. John, no! You can't go out there!'

'I've got to. I've got to get her —'

'You'll never make it back in time! John — thirty seconds! We've got to get downstairs!'

'I've got to get her!' He flung open the door.

'John, listen to me — *listen* to me — you *can't!* She's gone, John, she's gone.' She was sobbing. Her hands were on his chest. 'I'm more important — listen! I'm your wife, I'm *more important*. We can make another. I can't do it without you, oh, God, John, we can make another.' They held each other so tight that it hurt.

Molly, he screamed. Molly.

In the tree house, Molly moved her thumb around the device, turning up the volume. Where *are* you, Daddy? she thought. Rocket man! Molly liked the rocket man, burning silently through space. To Molly, he was a hero, her hero. She wasn't scared.

Rocket man, she sang, and the clock in front of her stopped.

Outside, the sky was malignant. The birds shrieked and wailed like mourners attending a wake. A veil fell across the once-blue Earth; everything was silent. The temperature dropped rapidly. Slowly, the sound of screaming echoed around the countryside as everything began to freeze. Blood stopped moving. The birds fell out of the sky. Come *on*, Daddy, Molly said to herself as she tapped her feet in time to the music.

Andrew Jury's story 'Glenda' in our anthology All These Little Worlds *went down well with readers, and some said they were left wanting more. We aim to please, so here's some more: a good long story from Andrew.*

Exocet

Andrew Jury

My father was a professional snooker player back in the late seventies. He never won any ranking tournaments, but for a while he was a genuine contender. He even had a nickname: The Exocet. Ernie 'The Exocet' Evanson. Not that he was really that fast. This was, remember, a time when most players took five minutes to make even the simplest-looking shots, and all the participants looked like Bill Haley's Comets in late middle age. He qualified for the final stages of the world championship four years running, and it was during the last of these years that he made the semi-finals, the high point of his career.

I was six years old at the time, and for a while, I was almost as popular as he was. Each time he won a match, I'd charge down the steps and leap into his waiting arms, and he'd parade me around the table, kissing me on the top of my head. The audience used to lap it up. It seemed glamorous at the time, but looking back, they were mostly grannies and fat older men. You can see for yourself.

Between matches on the television, they occasionally replay the old footage, and there I am again, complete with bow tie and pudding bowl haircut.

I even had a nickname of my own: 'Little Jimmy Connors'. That shows you how long ago it was.

These days, my father has a habit of turning up when I least expect him to, and at the worst possible times. Usually there is some unfolding crisis in my life. He will show up at a barbecue the day after my boss fires me, or be sitting on my doorstep when we return from the hospital after the diagnosis of our eldest son's latest illness. I think he times his visits to coincide with these traumatic moments in my life. I think he thinks it softens the blow. I prefer not to believe this. That would suggest he is watching over me, like some feckless guardian angel. Usually he is just after money, or a place to stay, though not always.

The last time he showed up, Wendy and I were in the conservatory, arguing about the furniture. I guess the specific crisis in my life was our marriage, only I was too involved in its decline to realise it at the time. He was holding a small suitcase in one hand and his cue case in the other. He never went anywhere without his cue, even now.

'Kevin let me in. He said it would be okay.'

'Oh, he did, did he?'

'Jim!' said Wendy, and gave me a look.

Kevin was my youngest son; young enough to believe my father was still the 'coolest old geezer on the planet'.

'If this is a bad time...'

Wendy shook her head and stepped forward to give my father a hug. She'd always had a soft spot for him, even at the worst times. To her, he was a rogue from a different era she could afford to indulge because I was the one who always picked up the tab.

'I have to go, Ernie. We'll talk later,' she said, and though she said it to my father, I knew those last words were really meant for me.

Alone together, neither of us could think of much to talk about. He said some nice things about Wendy and Kevin, and then he asked after Mark, my older son. All the time, he walked around and around the conservatory, as if there was a snooker table in the centre of the room that only he could see. I told him everyone was fine, and deliberately avoided talking about anything to do with his recent past.

'Jesus,' I said after a while. 'Won't you just sit down?'

He looked at me and sat on the sofa. It was over that particular piece of furniture that Wendy and I had been arguing. With her out of the room, it seemed absurd now, though I knew that would change the moment she came back.

I was about to ask him what he wanted, when he said:

'You seem surprised to see me.'

'What do you expect? It's been what, two, two and a half years?'

'Didn't you get my letter?'

I stared at him.

'You didn't get my letter.'

He frowned and ran a hand through his thinning hair, then closed one eye, a familiar gesture from his playing days. Back then, it was usually the prelude to some souped-up shot that would make the crowd gasp or the commentator wince.

'It was all in the letter,' he said.

'The letter. When have you ever sent me a letter?' I asked him. 'So what is it this time? You need a place to stay? Out of the question.'

'I need your help.'

'You're broke again. You need money...'

He nodded, but it wasn't because he needed money. It was just a nervous thing. It was two years since his last visit, but he looked a decade older.

'I wish you'd got my letter first,' he said. 'I sent it first class.'

'Why didn't you just call? What was so hard to say that you had to write it down first?'

'I've got this disease in my eyes,' he said. 'It's affecting my vision. They say it's going to make me blind.'

It was a degenerative condition. The poet Milton probably had the same thing. That was the way my father said it, 'The poet Milton probably had the same thing, Jimmy,' as if he'd had to memorise it on the way over. It sounded like something a well-read doctor or ophthalmologist had told him to put him at ease.

We were sitting at the kitchen table drinking milk. Wendy was still out. She hadn't said where she was going and she hadn't told me when she would be back. Mark was staying over with a friend. Kevin was in the front room watching cartoons on a satellite channel. Every few minutes, he would come into the kitchen to get a glass of cola or an ice lolly, but really he just wanted to get a closer look at his grandfather. Each time this happened my father would turn into 'The Exocet' and say something funny that would make Kevin roar with laughter. I mean really, genuinely funny. He could make Kevin laugh in a way I never could, in a way that had always made me feel relieved rather than envious. For the past few weeks, Kevin had worn a hunted look, the look of someone who was already starting to fray at the edges. I had thought it was something to do with school, bullying, perhaps, or some problem with his homework, but lately I had realised it was us: Wendy and I. Anyone who made him laugh the way my father could had my blessing.

'He looks like me at the same age,' my father said now.

'God, don't say that.'

'It's true. You see the way his hair curls up at the nape? And that bump at the top of his nose,' he said, feeling the gristly nub at the bridge of his old man's beak. 'I never noticed it the last time I was here.'

It was true. I didn't look remotely like my father or my son, and yet the two of them were the before-and-after image of each other.

'What's he like with a cue in his hand?'

'Don't even think about it,' I said.

'I was just asking.'

'He's a blank page. Incorruptible.'

'You don't let him play?'

'He's never asked,' I said. 'Change the subject, will you?'

My father sighed and rubbed his hand along the cue case. His suitcase was under the table. There was a tag on the handle with his name on it and an address for a bed and breakfast in Margate. I could picture it: Ernie Evanson. *The Exocet*. Still Alive Tour: 7pm. The air thick with smoke, the lights so low it felt like you might get the bends just standing there in the dark. A few trick shots, some banter with the audience, then down to the fake nitty-gritty: a century break, the balls cunningly positioned. 'Exhibition stuff.' And then the final black...with some quick joke at his own expense before the wag at the back made it for him.

'So what are you going to do?' I asked him.

'What else? Make the most of whatever time I have left.'

'Can't they reverse it? Slow it down?'

'They're not sure. I don't think so. There are some things they can do and some things I can do, apparently.' He shrugged. 'They're just playing doctors. The damage is done.'

'So what caused it? Do they know?'

'It's not genetic, if that's what's bothering you.'

'That's not what I meant.'

'Even if it was, it's Kevin you'd have to worry about. Everything skips a generation. You only have to look at him to know that.'

'He isn't you, dad. He's never going to be you.'

'No, he's the best of me. With all the finer parts of his mother thrown in for free.'

'Don't I get a look in?'

'Ha! You shouldn't be so hard on yourself,' he said. 'You're a good father, Jimmy. A good husband.'

He was fishing. Letting me know that he knew something was wrong. What did he think? That I might pour my heart out to him? Think again, Exocet.

'You can't stay here,' I said again.

'Is it an inconvenient time for you?'

I sighed.

'What's that for?' he asked me.

'The way you do that.'

'Do what?'

'Try to be subtle, when we both know you'll just come out and say it anyway.'

'I wasn't trying to be anything. I just want a roof over my head for a few days.'

'A few days...'

He smiled. 'I suppose it could be longer.'

I shook my head.

'Is that a resigned shake of the head? A last rueful act of defiance?'

'It's not a joke, I'm serious. You can't stay.'

If this were a movie, the next scene would be him moving his stuff into the spare room. Sitting with his feet up on the credenza, if we had one, and chalking the tip of his cue...

'What will you do if I say no?'

He took a swig of milk, and then poured himself another glass. 'I'll go over your head. Appeal to a higher power.'

I said, 'Wendy.'

'She'll give me the green light, guaranteed, and then you'll have to explain to her why you said no in the first place. And that's another small bone of contention between the two of you right there.'

I shook my head again. 'You're a slick old fucker, I'll give you that. You had this all planned out, didn't you?'

He gave me an old look, what he called his 'innocent abroad' expression.

'You should have got the letter,' was all he said.

Later that night, he suggested we go out for a drink.

My father is a recovering alcoholic; he's been recovering for almost thirty years now. I didn't say anything, but he could tell by the look on my face that I didn't think it was such a good idea.

'You never could hide your true feelings from me,' he said, laughing.

'What about your —'

'I haven't touched a drop in over five years. Anyway, it's not me I'm thinking about. You're the one who looks like he needs some cheering up.'

Wendy didn't mind. At any other time, she might have protested, but I think she was glad to have us out the house. She'd only been back a few minutes, but wherever she'd been, it hadn't changed the way she felt about me. She made small talk with my father, but I could see that her mind was elsewhere; for once, the old Exocet charm had failed to completely bowl her over. Eventually, my father got the message and went upstairs to freshen up.

'So he's staying, is he?' she asked me.

We were in the kitchen, where most of our arguments seemed to end one way or another.

'He says he is.'

She looked away, began making herself a sandwich.

'I thought you wouldn't mind.'

'I don't,' she said. 'Actually, that's not right. I don't really care.'

This was not like her at all. Whatever else was happening in her life, it usually wasn't enough to colour her feelings for my father. She'd always been prepared to make an exception for him, perhaps because he added a touch of salty glamour to our lives.

She said, 'Just make sure you don't give him any more money.'

'You know about that?'

'Jim, we're not so well off that I don't notice.'

I'd been about to tell her about his condition, but now I changed my mind. My father hadn't said anything about keeping it a secret from the rest of the family, but right then I didn't want her to know.

'I don't think he wants a handout this time.'

'He's not in any trouble, is he?'

'No, I don't think so. At least, he hasn't said anything to me.' Then: 'Ask me again later.'

The pub was within walking distance. I guess it was close enough to be my local, though I didn't really know the regulars well enough except to say hello to one or two of them. It was different with my father. As soon as we came in, the whole atmosphere changed. It didn't matter that it was almost three years since he'd last set foot in the place. They still treated him as if he were one of their own.

Ernie 'The Exocet' Evanson.

They couldn't get enough of him.

It had taken me almost forty years not to be bothered by this kind of thing anymore.

By the time we got a table to ourselves, we were up to our third round, and neither one of us had needed to put a hand in his pocket. I was drinking bitter. He was on his third pint of orange juice. He asked me about Kevin and Mark. He said they were great kids, and I stopped myself from saying, Yeah, but how do you know? He told me he wanted to spend more time with them before...well, you know...and here he pointed to his head and twirled his fingers, crossing his eyes.

'You're losing your sight, not your mind.'

'What's the difference?'

I said, 'Just about everything.'

He took a sip of his drink. 'I was thinking of getting one of those blind dogs. Training him up.'

'They call them "seeing eye dogs".'

'And an armband that glows in the dark.'

'What about a pair of dark glasses?'

'Roy Orbison style?'

I nodded, straight faced.

'I met him once at a charity do. Nice fellow.'

'Now you're taking the piss.'

I laughed, though it was hard to be sure if he was kidding or not.

'Have you told Wendy?' he asked me.

'Not yet.'

'I don't want you telling the boys.'

'They'll have to know at some point.'

I could see their faces already: blank indifference on Mark's (he'd never really seen the point of grandpa); incredulity, perhaps even a flare of anger on Kevin's. You could never be sure with him. He got upset and felt betrayed by the smallest things, like the time I told him there were some birds that couldn't fly. It's okay, I tried telling him, they're the exception to the rule; which just made him cry even harder.

'Tell them after the fact,' he said. 'At least that way I won't have to see their faces.'

We were quiet for a moment. The men at the bar were talking in loud voices. I heard the word 'Exocet' and the name of an old rival in the same sentence. More laughter. One or two of them looked over at us, though I couldn't quite read their expressions. I hoped none of them came across.

I was starting to feel a little drunk.

He said, 'Did you read that article about me?'

'Which article?'

'The one in the *Sunday Express*.'

I continued to play dumb.

'It was a full spread. Main feature. You're telling me you didn't see it?'

'Oh, that one. I read it, yes.'

'The kid they sent to interview me...' He shook his head. 'I started talking about the cue ball and the object ball and he looked at me as if were speaking in riddles. And his questions...'

I nodded, not really listening. A friend of mine had shown me the article. It was one of those 'Where are they now?' pieces. It was obvious that the reporter had wanted my father to talk about the drink and the drugs, like he was angling for a retrospective exposé of a time and place no one cared about any more. All my father wanted to do was talk about me, about what a great son I was, 'then and now.' It was embarrassing, excruciating stuff: the written equivalent of him parading me round the table after one of his victories. On and on it went. There was even a picture of me from that time, sitting on my father's knee, some trophy in my lap. I looked like Mark when he was that age.

It was a relief to know my genes weren't entirely comatose.

'So what did you think of it?'

'You didn't tell them much about yourself.'

'Always leave them wanting more, that's my motto.'

I didn't have the heart to tell him it was a one-off; that there was never going to be any more.

'You told him that you were competing again,' I said to change the subject.

He nodded.

'Seriously?'

He leaned forward, whispering. The drink made me slow to react. By the time our heads were almost touching, I'd missed whatever it was he said. He sat back and took a sip of the juice.

'What?' I said.

'I'll need some backing.'

'I didn't hear you.'

'I said, I'll need some backing.'

'No, before that.'

He stared at me.

'Which tournament are you talking about?'

'I just told you.'

'I didn't *hear* you.'

'Which one do you think? The big one,' he said. 'The World Championship.'

'Ah!'

I said it too loudly. I was trying to focus on his face, but his features wouldn't stay in one place long enough. I wasn't like him. I couldn't hold my drink. In the old days, he would sink five pints of lager before the opening session of a match and still be capable of racking up a break of sixty or seventy by the end of the contest, though in later years he would puke up most of it during the interval.

An old memory: me standing outside the door of his dressing room, listening to the sound of him retching. Tap, tap, tap. And in I go to find him sitting on a stool, chalking his cue as if nothing were amiss.

A single regurgitated carrot sliding down the lapel of his waistcoat.

I said, '*The* World Championship?'

'There's only one,' he said, and picked at a small scab on his chin. 'I'll have to go through the qualifiers, of course.'

'Of course.'

I assumed it was the ghost of the drink talking.

'Like I said, the only sticking point is the backing.'

'So you keep saying.'

'If I'm to have a decent shot at it, I'm going to need a manager,' he said. 'And travelling expenses. Stuff like that.'

I smiled and looked around, hoping no one else had heard. He might as well have told me he was planning to orbit Mars in a homemade rocket.

'You want me to be your manager?'

'You?'

He looked genuinely surprised and I realised then what he was actually trying to say. I couldn't help feeling a little disappointed.

He started to say, 'So will you...' at the same moment I started to say, 'I can't...' and a look passed between us: two ships passing in the night. He stared down at his hands on the table. Shaking a little, or maybe my eyes were playing tricks. The voices at the bar were getting more raucous. I glanced over. It was a younger crowd now. Only a few of the faces were recognisable from earlier. I told him I needed a piss, and escaped before either of us could say another word.

The toilets were in a separate, shed-like building across a courtyard: three urinals and two cubicles. There was no one else around, but I still used the cubicle. My head was spinning and I put my right hand against the wall to steady myself. The bricks were cold and greasy to the touch, and my piss came out in short squirts, hitting the bowl like Morse code. I was only halfway through it when I heard the atmosphere change in the pub: some kind of kerfuffle, the sound of voices rising and falling like sirens. I knew even then my father was going to be at the heart of it. My piss was going on and on now, a golden thread tethering me there. By the time I got back to the bar, whatever it was had already finished. My father was sitting in the same chair and staring into space. An older man with tattoos on his arms I recognised from earlier in the evening had a hand on his shoulder, and then he was bending over and saying something into his ear. A few other veterans were standing around and shaking their heads.

'What's going on?' I asked the one closest to me.

'Drunks. Idiots.' He shook his head more vigorously and looked at the door. 'Little shits.'

He didn't say anything else so I pushed past him. People were milling around now, losing interest. Outside, I could hear the sound of raised voices. It was obvious no one knew exactly what had happened. My father looked as bemused by it all as everyone else.

'Hey,' I said.

The big man was still speaking into his ear. He had the look of a retired bouncer: muscles popping beneath his shirt like old bedsprings. My father was nodding, but it was just the nervous thing again. He said, 'It's okay, I'm all right,' to no one in particular, and then he saw me standing there.

'Hey, Jimmy. Where were you when I needed you?'

'Dad,' I said.

He shrugged the big hand off his shoulder and stood up. Then he leaned in close until I could smell his sweat and the citrus on his old man's breath. The big fellow stared at me over my father's shoulder and I gave him a small nod.

'What happened?'

He whispered into my ear, the same way he'd whispered to me about his plans to compete again. This time, I heard every word clearly.

'They called me a bottler,' he said.

'Who did?'

He looked down at his hands. 'They weren't even born then.'

'What do they know? They heard it from their dads.'

He pulled back from me. 'You know what they were talking about.'

I said, 'It was almost thirty years ago.'

'Might as well have been yesterday.' He shook his head. 'Thing is, Jimmy, no one made much of a fuss at the time. It was only later...'

He looked over at the bar, rubbed his forehead with the back of his hand. His hands were definitely shaking. I said, 'Come on, let's get out of here.'

One or two of the older men clapped my father on the back on the way out. Others shouted some encouraging words. It was like being a kid again, watching from the front row as another certain victory slipped away. All that was missing was the table. And the referee in his sparkling white gloves. Those fuckers. I always hated them. Like something out of the Addams Family: all slicked-back hair, hollow features and sunken eyes. Why didn't they do something? Throw their arms around my father, drag him away from the table, wave their hands at the other player in the corner: 'Over, it's over,' like a boxing referee at the end of a vicious contest.

Heartless bastards. All they ever said was: 'Quiet, *please!*'

And thereafter the relentless click of the balls.

Red, colour, red, colour.

My dad in his seat, rubbing his face.

'*Come on*, Ernie!'

Thwock!

It took him six minutes.

Six minutes.

No one had ever quite seen anything like it, he said.

That final black, he told me he wasn't nervous. All these years later, I still believe him.

When people ask him about it, he insists it's still the greatest break of all time, though I'm not so sure I believe that.

It was nearly the first maximum break to be made in front of the cameras, I do know that much.

Nearly.

Not the most spectacular, nor the most flamboyant break of his career. There was no playing to the gallery. No showboating. Just fourteen perfect reds, fourteen perfect blacks, the six colours, and the cue ball on a 'piece of invisible string tied to my fingertips'.

And the final black.

The way my father told it, the way everybody told it, he couldn't miss. To miss, he had to be trying to miss, and even then he still couldn't miss. But, he missed. It was one of those shots: either he hit it a fraction too hard or he didn't hit it quite hard enough, the experts never could agree. Not that it mattered. The black dithered in the jaws of the pocket, whatever your opinion, like a small animal gnashing its teeth: *Ratatattat*.

A pot, my father would later tell me, is like an assassin's bullet. Most times they go in, sometimes they don't. Sometimes momentum or gravity takes over. Sometimes natural laws are suspended...

...and sometimes the object ball comes back across the table and nuzzles the opposite cushion. Sometimes, in the moment it takes for a ball to fall or not fall, a father's life is decided one way or the other.

When I remember it now, it's like I watched it on TV. I hear the audience making a sound like a thousand people receiving the same electric shock, and the commentator letting out a masturbatory, 'Oh...*oh*...'

But I was there in the crowd. Sitting three rows back with my Uncle Charlie, Ernie's older brother (long dead now). The two of us in matching bow ties, like a ventriloquist and his dummy. Charlie threw a hand across my face, a moment too late, as if we were watching a gruesome scene in a horror movie. I remember in a cinema some weeks earlier, my father doing a similar thing with his hat when that head came out of the boat in *Jaws*. And just like my father's, Uncle Charlie's reactions were a second too slow.

What my father did next, what The Exocet did next: that's the other thing people always remember, the reason people still talk about it now. It was the Stuff Of Legends. What he did next was smile. My father looked at his opponent sitting in his chair, and he grinned. Then he turned to an overweight man in the front row and made a joke out of it; a throwaway line, something about how much that miss had cost him, because the money really didn't matter to him, at least not back then.

A few people laughed behind their hands, as if he'd made some risqué comment, as if they'd heard a tasteless joke about a celebrity who'd just died.

And then his opponent, who looked genuinely distraught, got out of his seat to offer his hand in commiseration. The Exocet put him at ease, smiled again, and the two of them exchanged a few words. Then my father left the auditorium and had the biggest shit of his life (he later told me). And when he came back, he lost the next nine frames and the match.

It was the semi-final of the World Championship. My father was the evens favourite. The papers said that he would do well to get over the disappointment of such a loss. They said if he wasn't careful, his career might go down the pan.

Back then, snooker still made the back pages of the papers.

My father never got past the first round of a World Championship again. A few times I've asked him why, if he wasn't nervous, and if he couldn't miss, then why *did* he miss, for Christ's sake! And every time he nods and tells me yes, there was a reason, and one day he will explain it to me, if I will just be patient. But as yet I still haven't heard it, and I'm starting to believe that I never will, or that he's full of shit, or else it's something the old ham is saving for his deathbed.

I didn't see much of him after that night in the pub. Although he continued to live in my house, he'd be gone by the time I or anyone else got up in the morning, and he would only return late at night, long after the rest of us had gone to bed. Wendy always left him a dinner in the oven. He'd sit in the kitchen and eat it cold with the radio turned down low, and then he'd creep up the stairs one at a time, so painfully quiet that each footstep was like the ticking of a bomb that was about to explode.

Every night, it was like waiting for your kid to come home after his first night out on the town. I couldn't get off to sleep until I heard the sound of his key unlocking the front door.

And then late one night, returning from the bathroom, I caught him standing there in the dark. I started to speak, but he put his finger to his lips and inclined his head towards Kevin's door, which as usual was very slightly ajar.

'You hear that?' he whispered to me.

Against my better judgement, I leaned in closer. Through the gap, I could hear Kevin snoring lightly in his bed. I glanced back at my father, who was looking at me with a faraway expression on his face.

'Takes me back,' he said.

'To what?'

'To when I used to do the same thing with you.'

I said nothing.

'Ah, you wouldn't remember, but I would stand there watching you sleep for hours. You'd make a sound like a train. You even used to whistle through your teeth.'

I might have been touched, except I remembered those nights in a different way. I remembered sleeping on hard mattresses in dank motel rooms, under stiff sheets that carried the odour of their previous occupants. I remembered lying on some couch or sofa in the back room of a crumbling old theatre, curled up inside a ratty blanket. I remembered the cigarette burns on the lino, the yellow and brown stains, and the threadbare upholstery. I remembered being awake after midnight in a dozen armchairs in a dozen foyers whose carpets always stuck to the soles of my shoes. Most of all, I remembered waking up the next morning with the taste of the previous night still in my mouth and the smell of hops in my pre-pubescent nostrils.

'Those were good times,' my father said now without a trace of irony.

'Yeah, I still dream about them too.'

'I mean it,' he said, sounding hurt.

'So do I. Now go to bed, old man.'

I don't know where he spent his days. I assumed he went to the local snooker club. He'd never been too proud to trade off his celebrity before. To be honest, I didn't really care. I had my own stuff to contend with: a wife who was spending more time away from home than was normal, a kid with problems at school, and another one with poor health.

Of all these problems, Kevin's seemed both the least and the most important, if only because I felt it was something I had a shot at solving. If my wife was having an affair, she was having an affair, and the only thing I could do about Mark's health was ensure that he took his medication on time. So when I was lying awake in bed, waiting for The Exocet to come home, it was Kevin I thought about. I even spoke to my father about him on one of those rare occasions our paths crossed.

My father said, 'The thing with Kevin is that he's a sensitive kid, just like you.'

Kevin had returned from school that same afternoon sporting a shiner under his right eye the size of a fifty pence piece. When Wendy asked him what had happened, he told her he'd fallen over on the way home and then run upstairs to his bedroom before she could ask him anything else. He'd stayed there without speaking another word for the rest of the night.

'That's your contribution?' I said to my father now. 'He's just sensitive?'

'Did I say "just"? Did you hear me say "just"? I said he was sensitive, just *like* you.'

He was eating toad-in-the-hole cold. Even the gravy was cold. I was sitting across the table in my robe. I could feel a draught from somewhere on my bare legs. It was almost one o'clock in the morning.

My father said, 'Are you and Wendy still at loggerheads?'

He said it in a way that suggested the two problems, mine and Kevin's, were part of the same deal; as if Wendy and I were the source material that he'd cross-referenced in another book.

I said, 'Is that why you've been spending so much time away from the house?'

He shook his head. 'I've been otherwise engaged, if you must know. Putting the finishing touches to one or two things.'

One or two things...

It was the closest either of us had come to bringing up the whole subject of him competing again. It was also the one thing I really didn't feel like talking about right now.

I leaned across the table and twisted off the end of one of his sausages instead.

'Toad thief,' he said in a companionable tone.

I chewed on the sausage and watched him eat. As a kid, I had always hated dining at the same table with him. He used to make these small smacking noises with his mouth, sounds that only a kid really notices. It used to drive me round the twist. I would sit there with my fists clenched, staring at my plate, feeling sick. I told him about it one night and he got upset and clipped me lightly round the ear, the only time to my knowledge that he ever raised a hand to me.

This might be unfair, but I imagine it coincided with a bad setback on the circuit.

Don't misunderstand me. He wasn't the kind of father who took it out on his kid when things went wrong, but neither was he the type who could put a brave face on a bad situation. I always knew when things were going 'bad on the baize', as he called it. I think this is why he purports to take an interest in the affairs of my family, even if it is mostly from long distance.

Or maybe I'm still that over-sensitive kid, just like my son.

I shoved these thoughts to one side and swallowed the remains of the sausage. Then I asked him if he thought Wendy was the kind of woman who was capable of having an affair.

He looked across at me, no doubt to check that I was serious.

He said, 'It sounds like I'm not the only one spending a lot of time away from the house.'

'Really. I want to know,' I said.

'The question you've got to ask yourself, Jimmy, is whether she's the kind of woman capable of having an affair for the right reasons or the wrong reasons.'

'You're saying there's a difference.'

'Anyone can have an affair if things don't work out a certain way. I'm saying that it's the wrong reason if you're the only one who's unhappy.'

He scooped cold mash on to his fork. At no point in the conversation had he stopped chewing his food. I'd once asked him why he didn't put his meals in the microwave, and he'd just shrugged. He told me that playing the kind of venues he'd played, and eating in the canteens he'd dined in, you got used to cold food. After a while, you even developed a taste for it.

Now I listened to the sound of him eating, and it didn't bother me one jot.

'So she's told you she's unhappy,' I said.

'You have to ask? You need me to confirm it for you?'

I pulled the robe tighter around my body and felt my legs going numb under the table. He'd polished off the remains of his dinner. There was barely a crumb of mashed potato or streak of gravy left to be seen.

His cutlery scraping the plate sounded very loud at this time of night.

I said, 'I can lend you the money, if you're still serious about competing again.'

I said it without thinking, to change the subject, or just to get a reaction. As usual, my father trumped me, this time by saying nothing. He tore off a sheet of kitchen roll instead, and used it to wipe his entire face. That was something else that always used to get under my skin. He'd do it when he was competing, too: wipe down his cue with a bright yellow cloth, before applying the same cloth to his face.

He told me once that he used a yellow rag because it might show up in the corner of a rival's vision; because of the possibility his opponent might be distracted enough to fluff his next shot.

Any advantage is a good advantage. Remember that, son. Every rulebook is just a guidebook.

His eating habits, they no longer bothered me, but the thing with the cloth still made me want to smother him with a pillow.

He said, 'Thanks for the offer, son. But I think I've got all the bases covered on this one.'

I said, 'Oh.'

And I thought, why did I say 'serious' like that? Why do I try to undermine him all the time?

He might have many faults as a father, but undermining his son has never been one of them.

He asked me if there was any pudding, and I told him there was a slice of apple pie in the fridge. As he went across to get it, I looked at the clock and thought about ringing in sick for work the next morning. Perhaps I could even persuade Wendy to do the same thing. I said to my father that the thing with Kevin...it probably wasn't that serious, after all. I would talk to him. I was probably just over-reacting. He looked at me as if he'd forgotten all about that, but then he wiped his face one final time and told me again that Kevin was a sensitive boy.

'I think we've established that already. So what?'

'I mean, it might be more serious than it seems.'

I had started to stand up. Now I sat down again.

'Have you been talking to Kevin too?' I asked him, my voice too loud.

'Have you, Jimmy?'

He poured half a carton of full fresh cream over his pie and took a bite. The hand holding the spoon was shaking. Either I didn't always notice, or the shakes came and went.

I was about to say something else, but then I heard movement upstairs, footsteps padding across a room. Whom had I woken? I had lived in that house for more than ten years, but right then I couldn't remember whose room was directly above the kitchen. Was it Mark's or Kevin's? Was it the spare room or the bathroom?

I looked back at my father. He was gazing upwards, too, and it dawned on me then that he had been seeing Mark without my knowledge. That he was seeing my son on the side.

I looked down at my bare feet and thought, I can't feel my toes. And I wondered how it could be that things had turned so bad on my own particular baize that my father spending secret time with my son didn't seem like such a bad thing.

My father moved out of the house a week later. My wife followed two weeks after that.

She is not having an affair, and she has probably not moved out for good, if only because she hasn't taken the kids with her, and because she is living with her mother a few streets away. As I write this, she is on her way to the house so we can take Mark to the hospital for his monthly check-up. They call the tests 'routine' and 'procedural', but I am always tense before each one, if only because Mark's illnesses have a habit of resisting such feeble attempts to categorise them.

Also as I write this, my father is preparing to compete in the first preliminary round of qualification for next year's World Championship.

Already, he is starting to lose his sight and has to wear special goggles to compete. His peripheral vision is severely limited. In the unlikely event that he makes it to the Crucible for the final stages, even the goggles may not be enough to enable him to take part. Still, he claims to be in the best shape of his life, which is not saying much. And he has a manager: an old pro from the circuit, another ex-alcoholic. And an agent.

I received a letter from him yesterday (a real one this time, unlike the one he claimed to have sent me prior to his last visit), in which he says there's the possibility of his own column in a local newspaper, perhaps even a book. What do I think of *A Blinding Success* or *Cueing in the Dark* as possible titles?

Not much, I will write back to him.

The tabloids have also cottoned on to the potential of his story. My father has enclosed one or two cuttings with his letter: 'Countdown to Exocet's Last Launch.' 'Veteran in Final Thrust for Glory.' 'Ex-star with Eyes on the Title.' Every article has the same accompanying picture of my father in his 'specially adapted goggles'. He's holding his cue like it's a spear and smiling, as if the whole thing is just a lark. His story is one of those dispensable footnotes to the real stories, human-interest filler. They probably have their final instalment already written, like an obituary.

At the end of his letter, my father says that Optrex is sponsoring his participation in the tournament. As yet, I still haven't made up my mind if this is his idea of a joke or not.

All of this, true or false, is dependent on him winning a few matches, of course.

The day before my father left us for good, I arrived early to collect Kevin from school. When he didn't show up at the gates, I went inside the building and was told by his teacher, a woman almost half my age, that Kevin's grandfather had taken him out of class earlier that afternoon. Some kind of family emergency, she said. The boy had confirmed to her that the man was his grandfather. And then squinting at me in a way that made me feel like the impostor, she said that it wasn't the first time. There had been other emergencies similar to this last one.

Was everything okay?

I told her there was nothing to worry about. I explained that my father, Kevin's grandfather, was eccentric, and that he sometimes got confused or else blew things out of all proportion, but otherwise he was harmless and well intentioned. I didn't say that my father had taken my son out of school to play snooker with him, or that I had been turning a blind eye to it for some time now. I didn't tell her that although I had not really known, I knew my father, and therefore had no excuse not to know. Then I thought I might tell her, after all, if only to put a dent in her by-the-book complacency, her smug *tell-me-if-I-did-wrong* satisfaction.

Instead, I made my way across town to a converted Victorian Cinema, itself an old converted jail — or 'gaol', probably. Inside, the smell of frying meat and last week's floor polish. Framed black-and-white stills in the foyer: Davis, J; Davis, F; Davis, S. In between, one of my father looking young and rakish, his bow tie hanging by its straps, shirt unbuttoned to the first hairs of his chest. They used to say he was the only player who ever made the game look vicious, a fight to the death. I always thought that had more to do with the extravagant follow-through to his shots than anything else: the cue like a ramrod, an exclamation mark to some fantastical ten-foot pot; his left hand pressed hard and flat to the table. The loose fringe flopping over his eyes.

All of his best shots looked like glamorous foul strokes.

Soon, all the kids were playing the same way.

Red, black, red, black. *Thwock!* Fuck *you!*

How many ruined cloths in how many snooker halls like this one?

Upstairs, there wasn't a single table going spare, even at that time of day. There were a few kids who'd played hooky from school, but mostly it was men of all ages with time on their hands, and too few excuses to play hooky from anywhere. No Smoking signs dotted the walls at evenly-spaced intervals, and there were glasses of freshly squeezed orange juice and colas on ledges bearing only the ghostly circles of old beer stains.

The old cliché of the smoky, boozy snooker hall was just that: a cliché.

The influence of the new breed. Young, clean-cut, health- and image-conscious: a TV movie version of real athletes. Or so my father would have me believe.

I took a few cautious steps towards the nearest table. At first sight, the other players all seemed to be concentrating on their own games. To a man (and one woman), none of them appeared to be interested in the old pro and his young protégé at the far end of the hall. But after a while, you started to notice it. Between shots, they sipped their soft drinks, cracked jokes and ribbed each other over their mistakes, but invariably their attention shifted to the end table, to the only game in town that really mattered; to the old gunslinger himself.

It was like a quieter, more reverent version of that night in the pub, before it had all turned sour.

I moved towards a pocket of deeper shadows well away from my father's table. No one recognised me or paid me any attention. Why would they? This was my father's realm. I remembered watching him as a kid, hour after hour, day after day. Every club the same as the one before it: the same décor, the same smells, the same Morlock complexions. This was my childhood: The Great Indoors. In every photograph from that time, I'm wearing a waistcoat and a bow tie, or I'm perched on the end of a table, or else I'm having my hand crushed by one of his grinning rivals. I remember thinking round about the time I stopped tagging along with him on the circuit — I must have been thirteen or fourteen — I thought: If I ever have a kid, it'll be over my dead body that he picks up a cue. Sanctimonious little squit. But still, there was my son, and there was the snooker table, and there was the cue in his hands...and here I was still thinking the same kind of things I had thought back then.

Had my father given him a name yet? The Small Incendiary? The Hand Grenade? The Starter Pistol?

I watched them for a few minutes. Kevin's face never cracked a smile. Usually, he grinned like a lunatic all the time he was around his grandfather, but not here. He sat on a stool while The Exocet was at the table, nervously rolling the fingers of his right hand around the cue in his lap. My father would prowl around the table and pot a couple of balls, before consciously reining in his old competitive instincts. A gentle safety shot would follow, the cue ball rolling sedately towards baulk. When it was Kevin's turn to play, he would approach the table like it was something not to be quite trusted, but also something that had to be faced down. He approached it, I noticed, with a kind of resolve that looked something like real contentment.

His cue was almost the same size as him.

Even from where I was standing, I could tell that my son had no aptitude for the game. I may not have picked up a cue in twenty-odd years, but I knew how to play; or at least, how others played. I knew real talent when I saw it, not that

I had any of it myself. My highest break? Forty-three. Three reds, two blacks, a pink and five colours. It would have been a half-century but for a bad positional shot off the pink: I put too much side on the cue ball, which left the white marooned mid-table and the final black tight to a cushion. The only possible shot? An audacious double. The black dropped into the centre but the white ambled off towards one of the baulk pockets. Foul shot, called my father, with a satisfied grimace. (A chip off the old block, I would later hear him telling his cronies.) Afterwards, he shook my hand and explained where I went wrong.

I was eleven years old.

(Another) 'one of my proudest moments': this one a direct quote from the article in *The Express*. To this day, I don't know whether he meant the break, the prodigal black, or both.

They didn't say much to each other, my son and The Exocet. Occasionally my father would make an observation, and Kevin would nod his head fractionally, or he would ruffle Kev's hair as he leaned over to attempt a tricky shot, but for the most part, there was no talking. At the end of the frame, Kevin laid his cue on the table and started to walk straight toward me. I took a further step backwards and turned my head away, and he walked past without seeing me. (Kevin could no more pretend that I wasn't there than I could pretend that I hadn't really known my father had been coming up here with my son during school hours.)

My father was racking up the remaining balls on the table when I went over to him, and very much pretending not to notice I was there. I watched him for a moment, and then went to the end of the table and rolled the other reds up to him.

'Is he any good?' I asked him.

My father finished racking the balls and I watched carefully as he placed first the pink and then the black on their respective spots. All the time, his hand was as steady as a rock.

'He'd need to practice a lot,' he said. 'But he's a patient kid. He listens. And he learns fast...'

He looked across the table and smiled. We both knew what he really meant. I just wanted to hear it from him, that's all.

What he really meant was, he's just like me.

Except that wasn't quite true, either.

I said, 'It's just a game to him.'

'Just a game,' he said.

I couldn't tell if he was disappointed or not.

I looked at his face beneath the glare from the overhead light, and tried to imagine him as a blind man: his eyes dancing in their sockets as he felt his way around the table, chalky fingers sliding up the cue to its tip.

Is the black still on its spot, Jimmy? Just tell me that.

Were there snooker tournaments for the blind?

That reporter, the one who didn't know his cue ball from his object ball: he'd prefaced his article by describing my father as 'having the kind of face that launched a thousand satellite tournaments.' Looking at him now, seeing my son's face buried deep beneath those downtrodden features, I could see that it was the one thing the hack had got right.

He said, 'Don't worry, this will be the last time. I'm leaving tomorrow.'

I nodded and spotted the three baulk colours.

'Are you going to be all right?' I asked him.

'You know me,' he said, his voice giving nothing away.

He wiped his hand on his trousers, picked up his cue, and examined the tip for the millionth time in his life. I sighed and tossed him the chalk. He looked over at the door and grinned.

'We've got the table for another hour.'

'Another frame,' I told him. '*One* more. And you never mention it again.'

He nodded. 'What about Kevin, you're sure he'll understand? After I'm gone, I mean.'

'I'll talk to him. And don't let Wendy see the two of you coming in together.'

'He'll be back any minute. He only went to the toilet.'

'Do you hear me?'

He looked at me and gave the thumbs-up.

'If he's not home in an hour, it won't be me you'll have to answer to.'

He chalked his cue and tilted his jaw at me, squinting, while all the time looking for Kevin out the corner of his eye.

He said, 'Jimmy...'

'Don't worry. I'm not going to ruin it for you.'

He nodded, clearly relieved, like I had just fluffed an easy red, and I took the fire exit down to the rear of the building. As I walked home, I tried not to think of him sitting in a chair somewhere, rubbing his face with a yellow cloth as some pastry-faced kid racked up another century break. Instead, I thought of what I would tell Wendy in a few minutes. I would tell her that Kevin was staying with his friend, and hope that she didn't ask me for a name; but of course, when I got home, Wendy wasn't there.

Like I say, that was a month ago. Since then, some things have changed, and others have stayed the same. Wendy has gone, Mark is still ill, and Kevin is back to something like his old self. In his next letter, my father has promised to tell me about that final black...if I still want to know. He says he doesn't want me reading about it in his book first.

Sooner or later, I will write back to him, but for the moment I don't know what my answer will be.

All These Little Worlds didn't have any debut authors, which was a shame. We're making up for it here with Ben Johncock's story, and with this one from newcomer Shari Aarlton. She's also our first author from New Zealand.

The Pest

Shari Aarlton

My sister was on the phone again. 'I can't stand it, Johnny. Andy's crying; isn't there something that can be done about that pest?'

I sighed. 'Not much, she's within her rights.'

'Andy's only six, she doesn't understand.'

Frankly, nor did I. 'I can write her a letter asking for the toy to be returned. But if she won't return it then legally there isn't much that can be done.'

'Will you write? As soon as possible?'

'I'll write a letter now, and drop it in her mailbox tomorrow.'

'Thank you, you're the best big brother a girl could have.'

I tried to be. But this latest problem looked as if it could be beyond any solution I could think of. It had all started when the property next to Karen and Jerry's few acres had changed hands. Originally it had belonged to an elderly lady who doted on their daughter Andrea. She'd been a sort of grandmother to the child, and an adoptive mother to my sister who'd been only twelve when our mother died. Our father had been a good man and a loving father, but when he died eleven years later there were only Karen and I.

Karen married at twenty-three. She and Jerry bought a property and started landscaping around the old house. She'd had Andy a year later, and that was when old Mrs Mannifree had come into her own. She gave advice, offered to babysit, and shared cups of tea with Karen whenever Jerry worked late. Several times when he was away overnight she slept there as company for Karen and baby Andy, and they adored her.

I sat down with my laptop and began impersonally.

> Dear Ms Boothman, your neighbour has asked me to apologize sincerely for her daughter's actions. Andrea is only six and when one of your dogs frightened her she reacted without thinking.

If only Mrs. Mannifree hadn't died, there wouldn't have been a problem at all. But six months ago she'd sat down in her big armchair before coming over to dinner with my sister and the family, and sometime over that next hour she'd suffered a massive heart attack. Her children had come home as fast as a plane flight could bring them. They'd gutted the house and sold the estate within weeks.

Most of the farm (and it had been a large one, the land rented of recent years as supplementary grazing for a local farmer's jersey herd) had been sold to a company that put in fruit trees, appointed a manager, brought in machinery, built a house and outbuildings, and, so far as anyone here knew, sat back waiting for the trees to fruit. Certainly no one saw much of the manager.

The house, and the remaining ten acres on two separate titles, had been sold to a Ms Hilda Boothman, a bland-faced lady of forty-plus years who bred dogs, neurotic inbred brutes that were nonetheless very valuable show-winners. We learned that she had independent means, that she valued her dogs above anything else; and that she had entirely her own way of dealing with anyone who crossed her.

> She was not on your property but beside the boundary fence when one of your dogs leapt at the fence barking and snarling. In fright Andrea flung her toy at the dog and ran. I understand you picked up the toy that was on your property and despite the requests of Andrea's mother, Mrs Mckay, you have refused to return it.

Typically mean-spirited, I reflected. Ms Boothman wasn't popular locally. She'd arrived with her dogs, most of which barked half the night and which were permitted to run loose on the rear part of the property. Miss Jansson, the elderly neighbour whose small house was close to the kennel block, had been driven to sell her home and move.

My sister was fortunate that their house was separated from the kennels by much of their land and the wide, deep band of trees between them. There'd been complaints about the number of dogs, but with the land on two titles Ms Boothman had a legal right to keep that many. Appealed to, the Animal Welfare Society said that the animals were well fed and housed, the Health Department said that the dogs were kept in clean conditions with all debris suitably disposed of, and her lawyer wrote most unpleasant letters to those who complained, threatening an action for slander.

The toy thrown by Andrea was a stuffed cat, and it was thrown in reaction to her fright and not in an attempt to harm one of your dogs. It is lightweight, soft, and could have done no damage had it even struck a dog – which I am assured it did not do. However it is Andrea's favourite toy, one she loves dearly, and she is deeply distressed at its absence. Could you please accept the child's apology and return the toy.

Sincerely, John Greville.

I had no confidence that she would. My sister, in her first attempt to get the toy back, had been told that it had been found on Ms Boothman's land, clearly as a missile thrown at one of her prize-winning dogs, and that she would therefore be keeping it. As backup, I spent time the next week when I had a day in the city court, in finding a stuffed plush cat of exactly the same appearance.

Karen phoned me that night. 'I had a letter from the Boothman woman while you were away.'

'And?' I waited for the other shoe to drop.

'She says that she will not return the toy, that it was used to attack one of her dogs, and if returned may well be so used again.' Her tone was an imitation of the lady's rather pedantic voice. The rest of the letter she read as if she were the writer, her voice becoming more and more bitter.

If one of my dogs should be attacked again I will have no hesitation in making an official complaint to the police. Any injury – mental or physical – to my dogs would reduce their value and quite apart from any criminal charges would merit a civil suit's being brought. I suggest that your child is kept away from my boundary in future.

Sincerely, Ms Hilda Boothman.

'What do you think, Johnny?' There was no doubt that my sister was furious, and frightened. 'Could she do any of that?'

I considered. 'Criminal charges are unlikely. No judge is going to blame a six-year-old that was frightened by a dog and threw her toy at it, even if it happened twice. But civil courts can be tricky. If she claimed Andrea was regularly throwing things at her dogs, if she took a dog with some minor injury to the vet and said that Andrea had caused it, if she had an animal behavioural expert in who said that the dog's mental state was being affected by this and that it was no longer doing as well at the shows because of it, then it is just possible that she could persuade a jury into an award of some minor amount.'

I heard a sound like a hiss. 'How much?'

'Perhaps a hundred or two. It isn't the award. Even the lawyer's fees might not be so bad. I deal with property sales, but I have friends I could ask to represent you. What you do have to think about is Jerry's reputation.'

'What? How?'

'My dear, he's a policeman. Imagine if the papers got hold of that. Headlines like, 'Detective's Daughter Ruins Dog's Show Career.' 'Policeman Says His Daughter Was in the Right!''

'So if she brought a civil case we'd lose, one way or the other?'

'Most probably. In my opinion the lady would do her best to see that the newspapers heard. If she brought a civil case, and you settled, she could tell a reporter it was an acknowledgment you knew you were in the wrong, and you'd get similar headlines.'

Karen's voice thinned to a wail. 'So what do we do?'

'Impress it on Andrea that she isn't to go near the boundary fence between you. That she isn't to speak to Ms Boothman if she sees her. In the meantime I'll be over tonight, I found a duplicate of Toppy for her. That should help.'

It did, for three weeks until Karen phoned me again. This time she was so mad I think she was spitting.

'That woman! Do you know what she did, Johnny, do you?'

'Not until you tell me.'

'Andy was playing with Toppy, she forgot she wasn't supposed to be down there. That woman looked over the fence and asked her where she got the toy. Andy said it was Toppy. That woman said it wasn't the real one. Andy said it was her Toppy, that Ms Boothman wasn't telling the truth. So that woman, Johnny, that woman went back to her house, got Andy's original toy, brought it back, waved it at her and said this was what happened to bad toys and stupid little girls. She tossed Toppy to her dogs and sicked them on to it. They ripped it to pieces in front of Andy and she's heartbroken and confused.'

I was flabbergasted. It was hard to accept that anyone could be so callous towards a small child. Why would any adult behave like that?

'What did you say to Andy?'

'I said that Andy has to protect Toppy. She mustn't ever go near Ms Boothman or speak to her again because she isn't a good person.'

'Will it work?'

'I hope so. She's asleep. Jerry got home in the middle of it and he's fuming.'

I got Jerry on the phone next and it took time to calm him down. 'Look, you can't do *anything at all* that suggests a private vendetta against this woman. All it would take is her making an accusation. Your superiors would hear the whole story, how you couldn't get Andy's toy back, what Ms Boothman told Andy and what she did to Toppy in front of the child. They'd be sympathetic in private I'm sure, but in public if there was the slightest hint that you were trying to get back at Ms Boothman for her behaviour, they'd have to censure you. They could even see transferring you as the easiest way out.'

Jerry went silent. Then, 'I hadn't thought about that last. I'll be careful. But it isn't right. Mrs Jansson driven out, Andy traumatised, people's livelihoods damaged...'

'What?' I asked sharply.

'Um, I shouldn't have said that. Forget I did, will you?'

'I will if you tell me about it.'

I knew he wanted to, and he might as well let me have the whole story. If I was keeping quiet about one thing, I could just as well keep quiet about everything.

'Okay, not long after she got here she went to buy something in Fordson's shop. She brought one of her dogs in with her, it snarled at a customer and he told her to take it outside at once. He says she did, and was nice as pie when she came back in. She apologised and gave him a large order once the shop was empty. He got that in, all expensive items, rang her to say it had arrived and she pretended to be surprised. Said she hadn't ordered anything from him, why would she when he didn't like dogs. He couldn't send the stuff back, had to sell it cheap, and he lost quite a bit of money on the deal.'

'Clever,' I said. 'No witnesses to her giving him the order.'

'Exactly. There's no doubt that she's a smart one. Her word against yours and a court won't normally convict on that. She did the same thing with Jim Tisdale.'

I knew there'd been gossip but I'd never heard the full story. 'What happened?'

'He's the one that built her kennels. She paid the instalments as they came due until the last one, then she said he had to put some stuff right before she did. He did that, did other bits and pieces she said needed doing, and added a storeroom. She'd not paid him the last five thousand, and she'd racked up another five thousand in extras.

'To cut a long story short, she got in inspectors claiming that his work wasn't up to standard, complained to the Building Association that he was overcharging, and they had to investigate. He needed the money, she'd made it clear to him that it could be years before he got paid, if ever; said she'd tell the Inland Revenue he'd asked to be paid in cash. He couldn't afford court so he settled last week, for the original five thousand.'

I whistled softly.

'Yes. She's a nasty piece of work.'

Andy got over her distress, Karen and Jerry made it a habit to avoid Ms Boothman, and things settled down. The orchard's trees grew and the company started spraying them. I walked down there and watched, having crossed the roadside ditch to stand leaning on their fence as the big machine rolled up and down, the boom trailing a fine mist behind it.

'Excuse me, sir. It isn't a good idea to stand there.'

'Oh?'

'Spray drift, sir. That's a pesticide we're using. Quite dangerous if you get too much of it on your skin.'

I nodded gratitude for the information and moved well back. 'A messy job. Hard work too, I imagine. I suppose you don't get a lot of time off?'

'Not in some seasons, sir, but once this is done I'm planning a holiday. Buildings are all connected to an alarm, one of the men will check on the place every night.'

I asked a few more questions, and strolled home afterwards. At least this bunch were good neighbours: no noise, careful about their materials, polite and pleasant.

It was three days later when the phone rang. I had just finished dinner and was relaxing with a glass of a particularly good burgundy as I watched a documentary.

'Johnny, oh my God, Johnny, come quickly.' I could hear screams in the background.

'Karen? What is it?'

'It's Andy, she's hurt, Jerry's away tonight.' The screams were mixed with sobs and cries of 'Mummy, Mummy, it hurts.'

I dropped the glass, yelled into the phone, 'I'm on my way,' and dived for the door.

I got to Karen's house just as she was bundling Andy, wrapped in a blanket, out of the front door, the child's face was covered with blood, she was crying and shaking from shock. Karen didn't look much better.

'Get in the back of my car with her. I'll drive.' Karen obeyed before I shot the car down their drive and along the road heading for the village. We had a cottage hospital there and a very good doctor lived in the village as well. I pulled up outside his house, leaving Karen to bring Andy, raced down his path and hammered on the door.

After that it was 'please wait here.' Once Andy had been initially treated, sedated, and tucked into a hospital bed he got back to us.

'I've called in two men who'll do a great job on her, they'll be here in half an hour. The theatre's being set up, and you're not to worry. Now, before they get here, can you tell me exactly what happened?'

I left that to Karen. 'I certainly can tell you. It was that woman!'

By now everyone in the village knew who was meant when the term was used. The doctor nodded. 'One of her dogs?'

'It'd dug under the back fence, and when Andy went out to play it jumped up and tried to grab her toy. She held Toppy up out of reach, and when the brute couldn't get Toppy, it bit Andy in the face. She fell over and it kept attacking her. I heard her screaming and I ran. I hit it with a stick, and it wriggled back under the fence. Her face looked awful, blood everywhere, how bad is it?'

Doctor Itubi is a kind man. He likes children, and they like him too. 'It's not good.' he was reluctant to expand on that until Karen pressed him. 'The facial damage can be repaired, however it may also have injured her left eye.'

And he was correct. The damage to Andy's face was repaired and even we could see that in time it would be invisible. Jerry stood aside; other police prosecuted Ms Boothman and her dog. She went to court with hired experts, and photographs she'd taken before we returned. They appeared to show that the hole under the fence had not been dug by a dog, but by a child with a spade. One picture showed scuffed ground on her side of the fence with smears of blood on the grass that an expert identified as Andy's blood.

Her lawyer cited the previous incident with Toppy and suggested that Andy had wanted either to hurt a dog in retaliation, or was carrying out childish mischief. That Andy had been on Boothman land when the original attack took place and that she may have provoked it: it was Karen's word alone that she'd caused the dog's injury with her stick. Ms Boothman was good, I'll give her that, she had the court convinced that this was an outsider being blamed because a dog-hating brat made trouble.

They swallowed it. There was insufficient evidence to show who or what had dug the hole, insufficient evidence to show on whose land the incident had taken place; but they leaned towards the evidence that showed it had probably occurred on Boothman land. The dog was discharged without a stain on its character and Ms Boothman walked out of the court with it at her heels, her eyes glinting in triumph.

She then went on to bigger and better forays against the village. One of her dogs on the road caused an accident, and she sued the driver for leaving a hole in her fence and injuring the dog. She said that when he damaged the fence and hit the dog, the animal had had been sunning itself on her land just within the boundary.

She sued a local shop whose owner had told her to 'take that child-savaging brute out,' when she came in with one of her dogs. It was admitted that she should not have brought the dog into a shop, but she sued for slander, saying that what was said damaged the reputation of her kennels. A credulous jury accepted that and she collected more than the shop-owner could afford, including paying costs.

About the time of that last incident Andy's eye developed a second infection where the dog's fang had grazed the eyeball, so that the eye had to be removed and an artificial one fitted. Before the time of the attack she'd been a happy outgoing little girl, now she was shy, nervous, and with one hand up constantly, shielding that side of her face. She wet the bed, and clung to Toppy as if he was the only constant in a shifting world.

I didn't blame the dog that much. Any dog left untrained and allowed to roam can be dangerous. It's the owner's job to see that it has training and discipline. No, I blamed Ms Boothman who'd lied her way out of case after case, who'd cheated decent people of their cash, and their character, and Andy out of an eye. Then she died.

She died abruptly paralyzed, alone but for her dogs, and since no one liked her it was days before she was found; and by then her dogs had become hungry. Since she hadn't seen a doctor in years there had to be an autopsy, which found that she'd died from pesticide poisoning. I was in the pub when that news came out and I nodded wisely.

'I'm not surprised. She used to run her dogs on orchard land whenever the manager wasn't around and even after spraying. Saw her there with them a number of times.'

Old Mrs Jansson who'd called in to have lunch (she'd bought a house just around the corner when she'd been forced to move), agreed immediately. 'Boasted to me once, she did. Said no one could stop her going where she wanted.'

Tony the builder added his mite. 'Think I've seen her there myself. Silly cow.'

Others piped up. It was agreed Ms Boothman had brought her death on herself. Her arrogant and continual trespassing, testified to by various villagers at the inquest, led the coroner to declare death by misadventure.

Ms Boothman didn't walk her dogs on orchard land, but I know people: if you say you've seen something, and say it with sufficient conviction, they'll start to believe that they've seen it too. The more so if it casts someone they loathe in a bad light. I'd read up on the stuff that the orchard used. I'd stolen a small amount of the concentrated spray from the orchard shed, and bought the sprayer months ago when I was well out of the area.

Since then, I'd been visiting Ms Boothman's kennels when she was away at shows and sprayed items that she'd be likely to use, then get rid of.

I went home from the pub and quietly disposed of the last of the pesticide and the hand sprayer. Once I'd cleaned up, I settled with a glass of good wine, switched on my TV, and smiled.

As a Britisher, I always find it slightly strange to read stories in which guns feature as part of everyday life, as though a crack has opened in the world and something exotic and distant has slipped through. I expect Americans feel the same way when they read about Marmite.

Trevor Gets Shot

Claire Blechman

I was lying in my back yard under the white pine tree, reading a note I'd snitched out of the math room trash, when Trevor came up and kicked my elbow with the toe of his sandal.

'Hey, Sean!' he said. I panicked and tried to hide the note, but he didn't notice. He had big plans.

'I want to get shot,' he said.

Yeah, okay, I nodded; but he meant it.

'Not in the head or anything. I'm talking a flesh wound.' He made a gun with his thumb and first finger and fired it against my arm. 'But not just a graze either. It has to be enough to mean something.'

Trevor's brain is like an amp turned up to eleven. He's kind of a legend around here, for all the crazy stunts he'd pulled. Like when he jumped his bike off the pavilion in the park the week before, or when he chased the train...Back in September he got Chrissy Gibraltar and her friend Janice to show him their boobs. I was so dumb I didn't see it coming the whole conversation. Then I didn't see anything at all because they made me wait behind the equipment shed. This plan was on a whole new level though, and it scared me a little.

'Dude, getting shot is serious,' I told him.

But that was the whole point, Trevor said. If it wasn't serious it wouldn't be worth doing. 'What's the point of going through your whole life doing everything safe and lame?' Trevor jumped to grab the lowest branch on the white pine. I couldn't reach it even with a running leap, but I'm short, and I suck at anything athletic. Trevor was pushing five-nine, and we weren't even out of middle school. He pulled himself up and over the branch. A piece of bark flaked off from under his fist; it almost hit me in the eye, and I flinched. I sat up so I could see him better.

'Is this because of Donny?' I asked. It happened to be the day after Trevor had finally convinced Donny to show us his scar. We'd been begging for weeks, and he'd always get angry and give us an excuse. 'It's a bullet wound, not a peep show,' was his favourite. They'd sent him to Iraq and three weeks later they sent him back with a purple heart. I saw him at the Memorial Day parade just after he got home; the cast on his shoulder was so big he had to keep his arm out of his uniform jacket. After that, Donny spent most of his time hanging around in the park, feeding the squirrels. Trevor and I would bring him an extra Mountain Dew from the Qwik Stop on the corner and ask how therapy was going. 'It's bullshit,' he'd say. I was always bugging him about the army, and he would talk about marksman training out in Greentop, or his buddies in his unit. But he wouldn't tell us the story of how he got shot.

Trevor didn't care how it happened: he wanted to see. 'Please? One quick look, that's all,' he begged.

Finally Donny agreed to show us, 'if it'll shut you the hell up.' He didn't even wait for an answer; he slipped off his jacket and suddenly he was completely shirtless, peeling off the medical tape that held thick squares of gauze to his skin.

'Whoa.' Trevor and I peered in close. It was a bulging red blob, with nasty yellow and black bruises all around. The last of his staples still ran like a broken zipper down his shoulder blade. I was amazed that your flesh could get so messed up and still heal itself. If I had to deal with a mess like that I wouldn't know where to start.

'Don't touch it, jackass,' Donny slapped Trevor's creeping hand away. 'So now you see, right?'

Trevor never answered my question about whether this whole idea was because of Donny, but it was obvious. Looking down through the pine branches, Trevor pointed out how Badass getting shot would be. I couldn't deny that. I asked him why he didn't join the army then, like Donny, and of course Trevor thought that was a stupid idea. He'd have to wait until he was eighteen. Trevor never wants to do things later; when he gets going, he has this momentum that builds and builds.

Next thing I knew Trevor had climbed down from the tree and was standing in front of me. His blue 4-H shirt had little brown bits of bark stuck to it. 'Will you help me do it?' he said.

'Do what?'

'You know, it.' He made the finger gun again and held it up in the space between us.

Trevor Huple's been my best friend since sixth grade, when my family moved here from East Hannibal. Dad talked for weeks about how great Clarence was going to be, a fresh start for all of us. I really believed him too, until the first day, when I sat down in homeroom and everyone picked up their books and moved to another table. How could they hate me already, I thought. Did I smell? I was wearing my best Batman shirt. How can you go wrong with Batman?

When all the other kids ignored me or called me 'that weirdo,' Trevor was the only one who gave me a chance. I guess he didn't care what people thought, because no matter how hard I try, I am weird sometimes. I say the wrong things. I trip on nothing and drop my lunch tray. I try to be friendly and instead I end up accidentally touching a girl's boob (which freaks both of us out). Deek Simons beat me up in the locker room because I hit him in the face with a dodgeball. He shoved me up against the wall and demanded, 'What's your problem?' I wish I knew. I wasn't even sure if I'd hit him on purpose or not.

'Sean?'

I could see Trevor out of the corner of my eye, with his face up close to mine, his arm leaning against the tree. Sure, we'd been on a ton of adventures together, but this was different. Instead of answering, I concentrated on picking at the loose bark. If you scratch deep enough, the sap starts to bleed out.

'Will you do it?'

Trevor was the only reason I could show my face in school. All the kids respected him, and not just for that pavilion stunt either. He was the one who pulled Deek off me in the locker room. Didn't even stop to put his shirt on all the way. It was still hanging around his neck, draped over his back like a cape.

This was a completely messed up idea, but I also knew that he would go for it whether I helped or not. I wasn't even sure why he needed me, exactly. So finally I said yes.

Trevor grinned, and shook my hand. 'I knew I could count on you.' He took out his beat-up Hacky Sack and started pacing around the tree, thinking. 'Does your dad have a gun?'

'He's a chiropractor...'

'But does he?'

'No,' I said. Trevor's didn't either. I had a moment of hope right there, that maybe this would be the one that he walked away from, one of those turning points in life like moving to Clarence was supposed to be. I should have known better.

'That's okay,' he said, 'I know who does.'

We walked up Shelby Street, toward the park. We used to ride our bikes everywhere, around town in big loops, but Trevor had broken his jumping it off the pavilion.

'Where is the best place to get shot?' Trevor asked as we passed the old armoury. He threw me the Hacky Sack but I bobbled the catch and had to go fetch it off the asphalt. I said in a hospital.

'No, dumbass, where on your body?'

I personally didn't want to get shot anywhere, not even in a hospital. But Trevor said I had to choose.

'Okay, then I'd get shot in the ass.'

'The ass!? Getting shot in the ass isn't Badass at all! It's like, embarrassing.'

'You'd still be getting shot,' I said. 'There's no important organs in your ass, so you wouldn't be hurt too bad.'

Trevor started listing people who'd been shot: Tupac, 50 Cent, Napoleon. Nobody cool had ever been shot in the ass. The closest was Larry Flynt (the *Hustler* guy), who got shot in the spine. Teddy Roosevelt was shot in the chest once and *finished the speech he was making*. That's Badass.

Trevor decided a bullet through an earlobe would be the best. That way, for the rest of his life, people would wonder what happened and know he was Serious Business. He started rubbing his ear while he walked. I wondered if he knew he was doing it.

I stuck my hand in my pocket, to make sure Janice's note was still there. She always folded her notes into this tight, complicated origami envelope. I rubbed the sharp corners into the webbing between my fingers.

Chrissy Gibraltar might be the most popular girl in school, but her friend Janice is the prettiest. She has this long brown ponytail that goes all the way to her butt. I liked to walk behind her in the hall and watch the way it swung back and forth. She smelled good too, like some kind of purple flowers, from this glass bottle she kept in her locker. She even sprayed it on her notes sometimes. I wanted to take it out of my pocket and take a big whiff. Not with Trevor right there, though (he'd think the other kids were right, Sean's a big fat weirdo).

Once, back in September, I was walking down the hall behind Chrissy and Janice, when a folded up piece of notebook paper fell out of Janice's skirt pocket. I knew it was my big chance. I ran to stop them, so fast. 'Janice!' I said, but I was so out of breath I couldn't get another word out. When she turned around I held the note up in front of her.

'What do *you* want, weirdo?'

I pressed the note closer, right up against her chest, but she squealed and jumped back. The note dropped to the floor.

'Ew, keep your hands off her, freak!' Chrissy stepped between us. The bell rang and I was alone in the hall. When I bent down to pick up the paper, it had a big dirty shoeprint on it.

Two periods later I realised they thought I was trying to ask Janice out. I was so embarrassed. Then I got scared that the note was about me, so I had to read it, though it turned out to be plans for Hailey Thomson's birthday party.

This note in my pocket was to Chrissy, but Chrissy had taken one look and threw it out in the math room garbage. She would be so pissed if she knew I'd read it. I had to snitch it though, because I knew it was about Trevor.

Two-thirds of the rumours you hear about Trevor were true, or at least part true. At the moment there were two going around: that Chrissy gave Trevor a blowjob by the equipment shed, and that she didn't give him a blowjob by the equipment shed, because he'd chickened out. Janice had written both on the top of the paper next to two lopsided boxes, and politely asked that Chrissy check one, so that 'the girls' could know what to think of 'W.B.' (which stood for 'Wonder Boy', their codename for Trevor). The girls didn't know what to think, and I didn't either. I couldn't ask Trevor, because I was afraid of the answer. Either he'd let that stuck-up bitch have him, or he was too chicken to get a goddamn blowjob.

We came to the centre of town, at the corner of Shelby and Chestnut. There's the Qwik Stop gas station with a mini-mart there, Vinnie's Pizza next door, and the public park across the street. Donny was on the same metal bench as usual, wearing his green army jacket, crumbling up stale dumpster crusts from Vinnie's for that squirrel with the chopped off tail he liked so much. A couple of pigeons were hanging around too, trying to horn in on the action. One fluttered in and tried to land on his bad shoulder. He slapped that bird away so fast it fell flat to the ground, stunned, and lay there a second before it came to its senses and flew off. The rest of the animals scattered when we came over.

We said hi, Donny asked if we had his Dew, all standard stuff. He unscrewed the cap and chugged the whole thing in under a minute flat. We sat on the grass and watched, sipping our own sodas a lot slower.

Before long, Trevor put on his best innocent face, the one he uses when he's trying to get into a place where he doesn't belong. He said he had a big favour to ask.

'What?'

'We want to borrow your gun,' he said.

'Ha!' Donny laughed. A few crumbs fell off his lap. 'No fucking way.' Then Trevor told him what he wanted it for. Donny reacted the same way I did, like he wasn't serious. 'No you don't.'

When Trevor insisted that yes, he really did want to get shot, I nodded.

'What have you got, a death wish?' Donny said to Trevor. 'You're too young for that shit.'

Last year in seventh grade health class, they taught us the warning signs of suicide: Giving away your stuff, making a plan, suddenly changing from really sad to really happy. I think about it sometimes, and I wonder how far I could get. I'd be totally obvious about it, textbook case, and see if anyone noticed, or cared enough to stop me. No one at school, obviously. Maybe Mom or Dad, but they were always wrapped up in their own lame lives. I tried to remember if Trevor had done any of that stuff recently. Did the getting shot idea count as a plan? He did seem really happy, but he was like that ninety-five percent of the time.

Trevor told Donny the part where he was only talking about a flesh wound. 'I can take it,' he declared. But he couldn't wait around for some insurgent to get him, not in boring old Clarence. He had to make it happen.

Donny called him a crazy fuck, a spoiled brat, and a few other names in between. Trevor got angry at that. He insisted that he wasn't crazy: he just wanted it to mean something, you know? He wanted to know how it felt. The way he talked about it, it seemed almost reasonable.

Donny said being shot didn't mean shit. Anybody could get shot if they're in the right place at the right time. 'That wasn't show and tell, you know!' He slapped his wrapped left shoulder.

'And you,' he pointed at me, 'you're just gonna stand there and let this crazy fuck get himself shot?'

I was all set to defend Trevor (not that I knew what I would say) but he spoke first.

'Fine. I'll bet Deek Simons has a gun; we'll ask him. C'mon Sean,' Trevor stood up like he was ready to go. I jumped up too, following right behind.

'Wait,' Donny stopped him before we got to the sidewalk. 'Don't go to some punk kid,' he said, 'you'll get your head blown off.'

Trevor turned back around. He thought about that for a second.

'Why don't you do it yourself, then?'

'What?'

Trevor was getting really excited now. Having Donny do it would solve all our problems. Wasn't he always talking about his marksmen medals? It would be totally safe.

Donny scoffed. Trevor never gave up though. He dared him. 'Are you going to help me or should I find someone else?'

They stood there for a long time, staring at each other. I was sweating just watching them. Donny's nose wrinkled. His jaw moved, chewing on nothing. Suddenly he whipped the bag of pizza crusts out over the grass. 'Crazy fuck,' he said. And with that Donny agreed to do it. He'd meet us somewhere secure, and he'd take his rifle and poke Trevor through the meaty part of his calf. Fewer arteries there. I thought it was odd that he changed his mind so fast but I figured he'd seen it in Trevor's eyes that he meant business.

Trevor had wanted to go right away, but Donny made him wait two whole days, until Saturday night. The wait was killing him, I could tell, the way he fidgeted at his desk all Friday morning. He wasn't in English class fifth period, and I didn't see him the rest of the day either. Sometimes he'd do that, skip for no real reason.

So Trevor was going to get shot and Donny was going to do it, and it was going to be all kinds of badass. But where did I come in? They didn't need me at all.

I'd been wondering about that for a long time, even before Trevor asked for my help. Once we were alone again on the park bench I got the courage say something. I opened my mouth and spilled it out quick. 'Why do you hang around with me, really?'

Trevor seemed confused, like why did I have to ask? 'Who else would have helped me?' Anyone else would have said he was crazy. Ratted him out to the guidance counsellor, he said. Not me. 'You're my buddy, Sean.' That's all I wanted to hear. I knew he meant it. And I knew I had to try my best to live up to it.

This wasn't going to be some stupid kids' stunt. We were prepared. We got gauze, and towels, and alcohol to sterilise everything. Black clothes, old sneakers, and a pair of safety glasses I stole from shop class. 'You see? I would never have thought of that,' Trevor said.

The alibi was my idea too. He'd tell the kids at school it happened going door-to-door for the Witnesses in East St. Louis. They'd totally believe it: people get shot there all the time. And I'd stand by his side, like I always do, Badass by association. I was really starting to get excited. It was going to be amazing.

His parents, we'd tell a different story. We'd tell them we were out in the woods when all of a sudden, BAM, he must have caught a stray bullet from a hunter.

When I first met Trevor's parents I thought for sure he was adopted. His mom wore an apron when she cooked, even microwave dinners. His dad was this shrimpy guy who never looked you in the eye (when he wanted Trevor to do something he'd always make it a question: 'Could you boys keep it down up there?') The Huples were Witnesses, which meant they had to go door to door and talk to people about how great God is, like travelling salesmen. They made Trevor go with them, until he said he would rather get shunned and scratch his eyes out. Their religion is so strict, they've never done one Badass thing in their lives. I guess they had sex once, because they had Trevor, but it was probably all vanilla, with Jeopardy on in the background, and at nine pm so they could get a good night's sleep for church the next day.

Witnesses aren't like regular Christians. They don't have Pastors, they don't celebrate Christmas, and they don't believe in hospitals. I don't think Trevor ever had a regular check-up. When he got scraped up chasing after that train, his parents took him all the way to Hannibal to have a Church Elder look at his busted ankle. He came back with a blue Velcro brace that he never wore except when his mother was watching. I wondered why it mattered what religion the doctor was, but when I asked Dad, he told me to mind my own business.

The Huples didn't believe in hospitals, and they certainly didn't believe in psychiatrists and Ritalin and all that. I'm not even sure if I do. Sure, I feel messed up sometimes, like when everyone is on my back at school, but some dumb doctor and his pills aren't going to do anything about that.

At dinner, my mother plopped down yet another tuna casserole (because they're cheap to make in bulk, she said). In Hannibal, there hadn't been much business, and Dad's practice went bankrupt. Not that anyone here believed in chiropractics either. We moved because Mom got an inventory manager position at the Diebold warehouse.

At Trevor's house on Chestnut Street, they'd bow their heads before they ate, Trevor's father thanking the Lord for the food, asking Him to bless practically everyone they know. They hold hands during grace, so Trevor drops his Hacky Sack on the floor and rolls it around with his foot. His parents ask him about his day, and he lies about everything. Even some of the little stuff that doesn't matter.

'Have you seen Trevor Huple lately?' Mom asked. I told her no.

Mom had run into Principal Wilmont at the grocery store, and the principal had spilled the beans about Trevor's pavilion stunt.

'What was that child thinking?' Mom wanted to know. 'Such a dangerous idea!'

'I tell you, that kid is not all there,' Dad said. 'And I'd hate to think what that landing could do to his lumbar discs...'

If they knew half the stuff Trevor did I would be grounded until my eighteenth birthday, just for being there. Trevor would never take that. Even if his parents tried to punish him, he'd say 'okay,' and do as he damn well pleased. He'd come looking for me under the white pine and we'd find some new adventure. Once his gunshot wound healed. Or who was I kidding, probably way before.

I lied to Trevor about my dad not having a gun. He never used it but I knew where it was. If I needed it.

Trevor's on top so much, it was easy to forget that he fails sometimes. When he does, he fails hard. Like when he tried to chase the train. The summer before seventh grade, we'd just started hanging out for real, like best friends. We were riding our bikes down Old Highway thirty-six, where the train tracks turn to cut out toward the river. Clarence used to be a big railroad hub, one of the biggest in Missouri. Now you can't even get an Amtrak ticket here. We stopped on the ramp to watch the grain cars lumber by, dozens and dozens of them. I looked over at Trevor for a split second, and all of a sudden he took off, pedaling as fast as he could. He ducked under the crossing bar and then he was racing right next to the train on that little service path. I followed him about a quarter-mile, until I couldn't keep up anymore. 'Wait!' I called, but he didn't slow down. Trevor stood up on his pedals, with the wheels still whizzing, and reached his hand out toward the access ladder on the side of the freight car.

I guess I don't have to explain how it all went to shit, and he never caught the train, and when he got up he was dirty road rash all over, bleeding from this deep gash on his ankle. On the way home, Trevor perched on my rear rack, his arms wrapped around my chest, and his ankle swelled so big he couldn't stand to keep his sneaker on. I asked him why he'd tried to catch the train. At first he pretended not to hear me, so I asked again. Because he didn't have a ticket, he said.

In the back corner of the garage there's this green tool chest Dad brought from East Hannibal. The drawer was sticky, so I banged on the sides to get it open. The gun was a Colt Army revolver; I don't know the year. The handle was ivory, curved into a flare at the bottom. It was his father's gun, which I thought was ironic since there I was running my thumb over the engraved initials while Dad had probably forgotten about the whole thing. If it had been worth any money he would have sold it to pay the bills. I dug through the pile of adjusting tools shaped like plungers, reflex hammers, and unmatched wrenches until I found four stray bullets rolling around the back of the drawer. Three I dropped into the chamber. The last one I put in my pocket.

Late Friday night I rode my bike out to the athletic fields behind school. No one was playing that day; it was just me and the motion sensor light on the corner of the science wing. It clicked on and all the moths were instantly buzzing around. I stopped in front of the equipment shed, where the track team stored their hurdles. I drew a target in black sharpie, an uneven circle about the size of a dinner plate, and stepped back ten paces to get some distance.

I held the old revolver at arm's length, peeking out my right eye. If Trevor got that blowjob, this was where it happened. Chrissy was kind of a slut. I'd imagined it so many times since I first read that note, but standing there I saw it like it was real. They'd have come right before dusk, after baseball practice gets out. He's leaning with his back against the faded wood and she gets down on her knees right in front of him, her face so close he can see her eyelashes flick up and down by his pockets. His fingers tapping over and over against his palm, like he does when he's trapped listening to his parents lecture on the Bible. Watching her hand close over the top of his jeans, the other slowly pulling down his fly.

The way I imagined it Janice is the one that has to play the lookout this time. I show up, and take her around the front, right up against the wall, and then...

When I finally pulled the trigger. I winced. *Click.* Empty round. At first it was a huge letdown. Then I laughed a little because I realized how pussy I was being. I set up again, looking dead ahead, pretending I was Donny out at the Greentop range for confidence. BANG the gun kicked in my hand. The bullet went wide, not even hitting the shed. I adjusted my aim to the right for the second shot. BANG, this one went just inside the sharpie circle. One more, I thought, to make sure it wasn't a fluke. This time I was cool; I didn't flinch at all. Dead centre. I was feeling pretty good about myself. Pretty Badass. I took the last bullet out of my pocket and dropped it in the top chamber. Then I stuffed the gun in my backpack with all the gauze and towels and supplies for tomorrow. Just in case. The motion sensor light clicked off as I walked home in the dark.

Saturday night finally came. We waited for Donny inside the back door of the old armoury – the one they were talking about converting into a lame 'teen centre.' Only the exit light was on, half burnt out so that it said 'xi' in orange.

Trevor had been thinking on the way over, he said. If Donny could manage it, maybe he didn't have to get shot all the way through. A graze would be enough after all. I wasn't sure at first, but I said if it was a big enough scar, then yeah, a graze could still be Badass.

'Yeah,' Trevor said. But he didn't seem convinced. Fidgeting with his hands, tapping his toes; I never saw him hesitate before.

To keep his mind off it I told him to remember that time on the pavilion. (He didn't hesitate then, not one bit.) Remember how it felt to be on top of the world, with everyone looking up to you, and that heart-stopping moment when you finally cleared the roof and hovered in the air, and you knew in another couple of seconds it would go either way, but you didn't know which.

'They made me go see the school counsellor,' Trevor confessed. That's why he wasn't in school Friday afternoon. Everything he'd done, and that was the one that finally made them notice? I asked what happened. He said nothing, he'd skipped. The counsellor was for messed up kids. The ones who set things on fire, or who heard voices that weren't there.

'Do you think I'm crazy?' he asked, a lot quieter.

And I had to say yes.

Trevor didn't say anything after that. We just sat there in the dark. I could hear him rolling the Hacky Sack around in his hand.

I'm the one who's supposed to understand. Be a good friend and see past what everyone else thinks. Instead I told him he was crazy. Not that I thought Trevor being crazy was bad: I loved him just like he was, a rock star and train chaser. I just didn't know how to tell him. Not without it being weird.

Donny was twenty minutes late. He seemed surprised that we were there to let him in. 'You still want to do this, huh?' Trevor nodded. The three of us went downstairs to the old firing range. It was pitch black in there. All that stuff I was carrying in my bag, and we forgot a flashlight. Trevor flipped the switch. The lights slammed on, one by one down the long corridor, like they were coming toward me. A single piece of target paper hung by one wrinkled corner from the wire across the back wall. The black outline startled me a little, because I thought it was a body.

The place reminded me of those abandoned institution buildings in horror movies. Scrap metal in a few small piles along the walls, buzzing fluorescent lights that probably hadn't been used in years. The backstop was a thick ramp of concrete, sloping up toward the ceiling. If I had come down here by myself I would have been freaked out for sure.

Donny pulled out a sleek looking black rifle from under his trench coat. I couldn't help asking what kind it was. 'AR15,' Donny said, 'Semi-auto. Custom assembled.'

'Is it loaded?'

'It is now.' He jammed a long curved cartridge into the bottom. 'You want to see what this thing can do?' We both nodded. Donny winced a bit when he brought the rifle up to his good right shoulder.

BANG. The target flipped over in the air then dropped splat on the ground. He'd blown away the clothespin that was holding it to the wire. It was the single most Badass thing I had ever seen.

'Are you ready there, Rambo?'

I gave Trevor my scratched up safety glasses I stole from shop class. We low-fived and Trevor went to the other end of the range. Donny knelt with his big brown combat boot toeing the black painted firing line. I must have had a look on my face, because Donny winked at me, and he told me not to worry. I felt better hearing it from a professional like him.

'Gimme a sec,' Trevor called back to us. His voice echoed. Trevor let out a big breath. He jumped in place and flapped his hands in front of himself, then at his sides. He slapped the ground, his face, each of his calves. 'Okay. I'm ready.' He put his hands against the side wall and extended his left leg out behind him, like a runner stretching his muscles.

BANG. Donny fired. It was loud, echoing off the walls. I blinked hard. In that tiniest moment when my eyes were closed, I saw Trevor make that landing from the pavilion, how the bike bounced out from under him and he just kept running.

I looked for blood. I waited for him to fall. But he was just standing there, like normal, and I had no idea what was supposed to happen next.

'Aw, you flinched, kid,' Donny said, like he was mocking him at keep away. 'Try to hold reeeeeal still. You wouldn't want me to bust your kneecap would you?' Trevor said he was sorry, he didn't mean to, but now he was twitching like a full-blown freakshow, pulling his leg up in starts.

'Trevor, seriously, keep still,' I said before Donny could hush me.

Instead he sat down in a heap. 'I can't,' he whimpered. 'Don't do it.'

He was chickening out. The one thing he wanted more than anything else and he couldn't go through with it. I wanted to run down there and shake him.

'Finally. Jeez.' Donny popped the cartridge out and flipped the cap down over his scope. 'Now you see! Not so glamorous is it?'

Then I realized that Donny never meant to shoot Trevor: it was all to teach him a lesson. 'Wait!' I called, just as he pulled open the range door, 'I'll talk to him.'

'No, son, we're done here. Take him home.' And with that he was gone.

Trevor was losing it. That was no Badass, crying on the floor. The blow job must have been only the beginning. It was all going to shit, and I didn't want it to. Maybe Trevor was crazy, but better crazy than this. I reached into my backpack and pulled out my father's gun.

When I got to the far end of the range, Trevor was chewing on his thumbnail. In his other hand he squeezed his Hacky Sack. 'I'm sorry, Sean,' he apologized. 'I'm sorry.'

'It's ok,' I said. I helped him up. 'Stand right there for a second.' I took a few steps back. I wasn't a marksman like Donny, but I needed some distance.

'What...' He saw the Colt in my hand but he didn't get scared right away. It goes to show how much he trusted me. I couldn't see his eyes very well behind the safety glasses. He was gripping that Hacky Sack real close though.

'Don't move.' I sighted carefully, made sure to aim low, and a little to the right. I didn't want to hit the bone, but I didn't want to miss either. It had to be enough to mean something.

Then he realized what was I was doing. 'No, wait! Sean!' He held up his hands, like that would stop me. 'This isn't what I want!'

'You do.' I told him. 'You just don't know it.'

It was ugly. Trevor's legs fell out from under him, before the shot stopped echoing off the walls. He screamed so loud it filled my whole head. I'd gotten his calf alright, but the bullet stayed in, at the bottom of a black and bloody hole. Trevor clutched at his leg. I kept packing on the towels: the blood was coming so fast at first I couldn't think of anything else. I almost forgot the gun on the ground, but then I remembered at the last second and stuffed it in the bottom of my backpack.

He only said one thing to me after, during that long ride down Chestnut Street with him on my bike rack. As I peddled I felt him growing heavier on my back. I told him to hang on, we were almost there, even though it seemed like we'd been riding forever.

'Trevor?' I asked. He moaned a little, so I knew he was awake.

'Did you and Chrissy...? I mean, it's okay if you didn't.' My shoulder was wet. He'd been crying, or maybe just sweating.

'Crazy fuck,' he whispered in my ear. I laughed. I'm pretty sure he did too, but I don't know for certain.

Donny was rummaging in the dumpster behind Vinnie's when we rode by. I thought he was going to chew us out real good, ten times what he'd done to Trevor when he'd first asked Donny to shoot him in the park. Instead he only swore one time, 'Jesus Fucking Christ,' when he saw the bloody towel I'd tied over the hole. He took off his belt and MacGyvered it tight as a tourniquet under Trevor's knee. He scooped Trevor up and carried him straight to the emergency clinic.

For a minute there on the dirty floor of the firing range I had actually wondered if Trevor was going to be okay. But when we got to the clinic, and everyone was freaking out, running around and yelling about how did this happen, I wanted to tell them all to relax. Everything was going to be fine. They took Trevor in the back room and kicked me out.

I didn't go home. Instead I rode my bike as fast as I could down the old highway and waited on the hill for the midnight train. It came early: I heard the horn blowing a few miles out. I stood with one foot ready on my bike pedal. Everything was coming together, and I couldn't wait. I felt like an amp turned up to eleven.

Harvey Marcus is one of two authors making their return visit to The Fiction Desk *in this volume. Harvey's last story (in* Various Authors) *was written in an unusual second-person form, so it's interesting to see how he handles a more traditional narrative style in 'Blind'.*

Blind

Harvey Marcus

I stood in the train, my bag placed on my lap, with the cane in my bag. I kept feeling it through the bag, toying with it, willing the packed, stinking carriage to get me home faster. It was so full that anyone still wearing their jackets couldn't take them off without annoying at least three people around them. A girl next to me rocked dizzily. She might pass out, I thought, but without water or a seat to give her, what could I do. Finally I reached my stop, and I slid and pushed through the people until I was off the train, and kept on pushing till I was out on the street and walking home.

In the kitchenette I put my bag on the counter and boiled the kettle. I made a coffee, then went into my room. I closed my bedroom door behind me, even though I lived alone. I set the cane on my small desk and sipped the coffee slowly. Somewhere a long dry rasp sounded, a hiss that grew louder in the room then faded away. I took another sip of my coffee. The cane lay there, being a cane.

The body of the cane was white, and could be broken down into four sections roughly equal in length, connected together by an elastic string running through the hollow centre. It had a number of scratches on it, with the end (which was red) for sweeping and tapping along the floor being more worn down. At the top there was a loop of black leather to put your hand through, and a black handle. Other than the fact of me, a non-blind man, having it in his bedroom, it was unremarkable in every way.

A few days later, I was sitting at my desk in my office, when my boss asked me to pick up some stationery we were running low on. We normally get stationery delivered in but I guess it was an emergency. I wasn't complaining: if they wanted me to get stuff for them I would. Any break from the stream of data entry was fine by me.

Outside, the heat was custard yellow, filling my nostrils and mouth. I was wearing a light T-shirt, but I just had to cross the street and it was already sticking to me. It was little less than five minutes to the stationers, but I still bought a drink to take with me, just to hold against my head.

I was almost at the stationers when a large woman wearing a pink tracksuit and dark black sunglasses came off a crossing and stepped in front of me. I bumped into her lightly, and apologised, to which she flicked a smile but said nothing, then walked past me in the opposite direction. I looked back: I don't know how I had missed her, the tracksuit really was garish. In one hand was a flower print hessian bag, and in the other a white cane, similar to the one I had, but with a ball on the end that bumped over ridges and the kerb as she swept it from side to side.

I turned from my way and walked behind her almost back to the office, before she turned off the main road down a one-way street. She's probably going to the park, I thought. She crossed the road, holding the cane out straight in front of her, then turned left along the park, sweeping the way in front of her as she walked, quick and confident. I thought she must have counted the steps here, or knew by the dips in the kerb where the turning was. Perhaps she wasn't completely blind and could make out when there was a wide open space rather than a narrow, closed one. She came to a bench, and without seeming to check if anyone was sitting there, took a seat. She was still for a moment, catching her breath (I was sweating profusely now just keeping up with her), then pulled a sandwich from her bag and ate slowly, facing the park.

I ran through what I had seen: she was sure of herself, walked quicker than many of the sighted people around her to get to her destination. She had even strides, perhaps because she was counting them. Now she was on the bench she was slow, deliberate, wanting to draw out her lunch break. I looked at my watch: my boss would wonder where I was. I walked away back to the stationers, looking back once at the lady steadily munching her sandwich, the highlighter pink shape of her solidifying in my mind.

I was already in the habit of carrying the cane in my bag by the time I'd seen the blind lady. It was a kind of token, not a good luck charm exactly, just something I wanted kept on me. I was not nervous about being caught with it either. It was an unreal thing for me to have, and this sense of its unreality made me feel secure. I would be in the pub with people I work with, and on placing something in my rucksack it would poke out slightly, white and utterly incongruous, but no one ever noticed it, or if they did they didn't comment on it, didn't pry.

I had this at the back of my mind the first time I used the cane. I was on the train, completely crammed in for the rush hour. As one load of people left, and the next came on, I took the cane out of my bag, quickly unfolded it, and held it by my side. I hadn't made a decision to do this really, it was simply an automatic movement. The train was packed with people, but no one seemed to have noticed me. Perhaps because the action of taking the cane out of my bag, setting it up and letting it hang easily by my side had been so without prior conscious thought or motivation, it was simply not a factor in what people noticed. Perhaps everyone was just tired and wanted to get out of this baking metal can.

Soon the cane was slippery in my hand, sweat and nerves making it wriggle in my grasp. My options were closed off: there was no way to put it away now without being noticed, and if I gave in to my guilt I would certainly draw attention to myself. I had to remain purposeless, exactly as I had when I'd got the cane out in the first place, or else someone would see me, and that could be unpleasant. I tried to think banal, empty thoughts, and remembering a test from school, tried to think of ten words with the third letter C.

I was still thinking of the seventh when the train pulled into my stop, and still with only half of my awareness (exceed) I moved toward the door, and people were moving out (eccentric) of my way, parting like the Red Sea at the sight of my cane which was now sweeping (excoriate) in front of me just as I had seen the blind woman do. I managed my surprise at how easy it was to slip into the role of 'blind man'. I looked slightly above people's heads for the most part, though I still stole glances now and then around me; I still had to direct myself after all. No doubt if anyone had inspected me in even a casual way they would have seen through me. But they didn't. I was a visibly invisible entity to them, warranting no more notice than the next man on the street, just another faceless blur to avoid bumping into or interacting with. They weren't getting out of my way but out of the cane's;

they didn't see me as anything more than an appendage to the cane. In this way I was able to pass by unnoticed.

A month passed since that first day walking with the cane. I had become by that point quite adept with it, and was completely fearless in walking around the streets. I had briefly considered buying dark glasses to hide my eyes, but never bothered. By then I was used to staring fixedly at nothing, using the top of my eyebrows as the anchoring point so that I didn't accidentally train my eyes on anything. Indeed I had lost interest in looking around me much at all: I had seen all of these things before I'd had the cane anyway, and any minor seasonal changes they might undergo didn't interest me. For the same reason, at home I was now able to function without looking at what I was doing at all. I only really looked at the TV now.

Soon after that first day, I handed in my notice at my job. It was not that I had hated the work: indeed, sometimes I enjoyed the blank tedium of it, the ticking away of minutes toward my next paycheque. But whatever was happening with me was incongruous with my job-life. I couldn't very well be using the cane on my commute to and from work, then be sighted again during the day: it would be much too easy for someone to find me out. I would either be one hundred per cent blind, or not at all. I guess I'm pretty stubborn when I want to be.

I had some money left to me from an uncle to get me by for the time being, and some savings besides, so I knew I would be okay without a job for a couple of months if I was careful. In the meantime I spent my time going for long walks around the city, down any and every street I would never have thought to venture through in my seeing days. To save money I was eating less, and combined with the walking after a month I was leaner than I'd been in some time. The walks themselves went on for miles, and

I rarely paid attention to where I was going. I found I could no longer get truly lost, in the anxious or frustrating way that I used to. Being lost was only a condition of not knowing how to get to where you needed to be next, and whilst I often found myself in completely strange parts of the city, since I had no destination, I was not truly lost. When I needed to go home I would simply find a bus stop and use a map there to walk back (never looking at it too obviously, of course), or occasionally would take a bus back if it was too far.

It was on one of these long walks that I turned off a well-to-do street down a very narrow, cobbled alleyway. At one point the two houses either side of it came so close that I had to sidestep through, my cane rattling the two walls as it bounced off in its endless side-to-side sweeping. The path continued through this gap in the buildings and into some undergrowth. I thought I must have strayed into someone's private garden, but ahead through the trees I could see a couple of benches with a bin next to them. The path was just visible through the undergrowth, and I followed it until I reached the benches, then sat down and caught my breath.

In front of me was a green, surrounded on all sides by expensive looking cream coloured houses. In the centre of the green was a stone angel leaping from a rock, around eight feet high, the whole circled round by a little wall, and it took me a moment to realise it was a dried-up fountain. It wasn't a private garden, just an ignored one, or else they would have certainly blocked off the path I'd come through. There were only a few others in there with me: an Asian nanny sitting on the grass whilst a little girl ran around her in circles, and a man wearing a fine business suit, smoking in a serious way.

After I caught my breath I took the sandwich and apple I had in my bag and began to have lunch. In the time it took me to eat half my sandwich the child ran around the nanny seven times, and the man stubbed out one cigarette and was halfway through the next. I ate the other half of my sandwich and the same pattern followed: the child ran around in circles with the nanny clapping and encouraging; the man smoked his cigarette to the stub and lit another, like we were all stuck in a loop. The man was gaunt, with puffy eyes and sallow skin: the classic office tan. He could have been anything between twenty-five and thirty-five. I finished my cheese sandwich and was halfway through the apple when the man stood up, paced one way then the other, then finally walked over toward me, with long, quick strides. I would have had to run to keep up with a walk like that.

He sat down on the other end of my bench. No 'Is this seat taken?' about it, just sat there. Which was fine by me.

'You are blind, aren't you?' he asked. His voice was dry and tense.

'It would appear so,' I said, trying to sound annoyed. Just a blind guy being asked a dumb question.

'Only I thought you looked in my direction a couple of times there. I apologise.'

'That's fine.' Neither of us talked for a while. The man lit up another cigarette, but smoked this one slower, more thoughtfully.

'I lost twenty million dollars this morning.' He said it as if reminding himself of something totally banal. I must take out the laundry when I get home. And I should pick up some milk on the way. Oh, and I lost twenty million dollars this morning. The man sighed. 'At least, that's what they tell me. Who knows, I may have lost nothing. I never saw any of the money, except on the screen. It wasn't mine, it wasn't buying things that *I* could use. I didn't know what it was buying if I'm honest. More money probably. But since they say that the wealth I handled and invested was real, and they say that a large sum of this wealth has disappeared into the ether, I must have really lost a real amount of money that meant something, somewhere, to someone. I've been sitting here trying to figure it out, but I can't get anywhere with it.' He took a long drag on the cigarette, and smoke dripped from his mouth and nose when he spoke again. 'A feature appears in the *New York Times* over the weekend, the director of the National Institute of Standards in Technology holds a press conference on Monday, the CEO of a Japanese software firm resigns on Tuesday, and some people I'll never meet lose twenty million dollars. You can't possibly tell me any of this is real.'

I didn't reply. The man continued talking without pause, a stream of stock options, short selling, quantitative easing: words and phrases that had trickled into my brain from the news, by osmosis I assumed since I rarely paid any attention to the reports themselves. I recognised the sounds coming from his mouth, had no idea what he meant. He was talking in the code of Finance, and if he had been talking in the code of Computer Programming Language or Biochemistry I'd have been no better off. The nanny and child left the garden through another exit on the other side of the grass. I let the man's words fill me up. The garden was quiet, subtly removed from the city, each house around it with its back turned. The sun fell exactly even upon every blade of grass. The fountain was a parched white stasis. Even the trees and bushes were stilled, neither tended nor running wild, just held as they were.

After some time the man finished talking, lit another cigarette, and sat for a while. Then he rubbed the back of his neck with both hands, clapped them together and got up to go. He asked whether I often came by this way, and I said I didn't, that I had no idea where 'this way' was. He frowned, then said he would look for me here again someday.

'Fine,' I said. I had nowhere else to be, I thought, and here was as good as anywhere. He said goodbye and left the garden through the same exit as the nanny had used. Alone in the garden, I was then aware of my hunger, the amazing force of it like I hadn't felt for months, as if my insides had been scooped out and replaced with an empty barrel. I picked up my cane and took the narrow exit through the undergrowth. If I stayed much longer I would have eaten the soil, the stones.

I returned to the gardens every day, coming the same way and sitting in the same spot as before. There were never more than a handful of people there, even at the weekend. It was as if most of the city had forgotten this little area. Once I went over to the fountain, and saw in the bottom a number of coins crusted over with algae, baked into the stone. I saw the nanny and child most days, and once she smiled and nodded at me, then laughed when she realised I couldn't see her.

Ten days passed in this way, when finally the man returned to the park. I scarcely recognised him: he wore a white cotton shirt, jeans and flip-flops, a large pair of sunglasses and had the beginnings of a tan. There was no hesitation this time: he came right over and sat next to me on the bench. 'You're here,' he said. 'I wasn't sure you would be. But here you are. A good thing too.' I nodded: here I was. 'To be honest, I've hardly had time to think about coming back. Talking to you...I've never opened up to anyone like that before. Thank you,' he said, grabbing my hand and shaking it, 'thank you.' He got out his wallet. He handed me over some paper, money I presumed. I kept my eyes staring upward at nothing. 'It's the least I owe you,' he said. Even though I hadn't had a job for almost two months, I hardly spent anything and still had some savings left. I told him I didn't need any money but he didn't listen, so to keep him happy I put the money in my bag where my lunch had been.

The man seemed satisfied with this, then got up to go again. As he did, he signalled to another person in the garden: a different man I hadn't noticed before who was sitting on one of the other benches across the lawn. He was older, in his late forties, showing a middle-age spread beneath his nice suit. His top button was undone and he looked pale, squinting in the light like he'd not seen the sun for weeks. Before he reached us the younger man said goodbye and walked off, exiting on the other side of the green as before and nodding to the older man as he passed him. The older man took his place on the bench and considered me for a while. I said nothing, fixing my eyes as always on a blank spot in the sky, turning my folded-up cane between my hands. 'My colleague,' he began eventually, feeling the awkwardness as I was, 'told me about you. How you helped him after that week.'

I told him that I wasn't aware that I'd done anything special, that he'd sat next to me and talked, and if that had helped then it was down to him, not me.

For a moment the man didn't say anything. 'After that week,' he said, '*That week*, you must have done something. You wouldn't believe it if you saw it. It was...unreal. I've been doing this for nearly twenty years, and I've never seen anything like it.' And so he went on, a stream of words and ideas about which I could only glimpse the meaning: world markets, import and export trades, relationships and forces inexplicable to me, though, if what the man said was true, they were governing mine and everyone else's lives in thousands of discrete, indirect ways. He said that every year since he'd started working at the company, he'd promised himself he would leave. Just one more bonus, he'd thought, and he would be free, to be a teacher or start his own small business. As before I only half-listened to the man, just dipping my head down slightly so I could keep my focus on the stone angel ahead of me, the man's voice now nothing more than a drone, a static buzz of worry and regret. Finally, after a long time listening to him in this semi-conscious state, the man talked himself out, like a car engine sputtering to a halt as it ran out of fuel. He bowed his head and let out a little sob, barely a hiccup, then took a long deep breath and without a word got up, and left the garden.

I was alone once more; as before, a furious hunger hollowed me out, voiding my body from the feet upwards. I got up, unfolded the cane, and left through the alleyway. I found a Japanese restaurant nearby, and ate two bowls of spicy chicken miso ramen, with lots of soy sauce, four spring rolls, a plate of steamed vegetable dumplings, and two bottles of beer. The waitress could hardly believe how much I put away. 'It must run right through you,' she said. I was as lean as ever, it was true. When the bill came I reached into my bag and left one of the fifties the young man had given, and left without waiting for the change. The waitress called after me, 'Sir! Do you know that you left a fifty? Sir!'

After that day a new routine took shape. I would go to the park and sit on the bench. Sometimes it would just be me, in which case I ate my lunch there and left to wander around the city at leisure. The other times I would be met by one of the people I had talked to before, who would thank me, give me a sum of money, and then introduce me (though never by name) to another person, invariably a colleague or workmate. They were almost always investment bankers, though some came from other areas of the financial sector. Most were men, though again occasionally a woman would sit next to me. This happened at least once a week, though often two or three times. When it rained I sat outside with an umbrella, and they sat next to me under their own.

Days after meeting them, the person would return, always with a new 'client', and before leaving always pressed some money into my hands, anything between £200 and £1,000 in cash. I hardly spent any of the money. Occasionally I bought new clothes and shoes when they got worn out from my long walks, and I bought food and paid rent as before, but these things didn't come close to using up the money I was earning. I kept the rest in an old shopping bag under my bed, putting it out of my mind.

The hunger was there too, and after the talks I would rush to the Japanese restaurant and order a large meal for myself. The pangs didn't decrease in power the more I had them: the opposite in fact, as I found it more and more difficult to fill myself up, and soon I was ordering preposterous banquets. I never put on any more weight either, and in fact struggled to keep the weight that I had. The staff would rush over to serve me as soon as I came in. I tipped well.

It was a damp autumn day when I met a middle-aged woman in the park. Like all the others she started by checking to see that I was blind, then after the initial awkwardness began the talk I had grown familiar with. We were just getting started, with me settling my eyes on the dried fountain, when the woman broke off. I flinched: no one had finished so quickly before, or so suddenly, and no sooner had the fact registered than the woman stood up and half-walked half-ran around the fountain, crouching behind it for a moment, then ran out through the exit.

On the other side of the fountain a man was walking towards me. He wore a pale suit, had white hair, and black, ink-dot eyes. He was at once completely ordinary and completely unsettling, the kind of man you would fail to notice on an empty train, but once you saw him, or rather, once you knew of his presence, the truth of him was undeniable. In spite of myself I was not able to keep my eyes away from his, and I even turned my head when he sat down next to me. It would have been hopeless trying to fool this man into thinking I was blind. Only a truly blind man could have turned the other way.

Those two black dots were the first eye contact I'd had in almost four months, but they were less eyes than wells, empty and echoing. The man looked down at the cane on my lap, then back up to me and smiled. He sat back and crossed his legs.

'Allow me to say a few things,' he began, his voice even, blank, like a prerecording, 'and then we can see where we are. You can call me Mr White.' I told him my name. 'Good, good,' he said. 'You're in a bit of trouble, I'm afraid, and I personally am sorry about that. You are trying to help people, to make an honest living out of helping them. This business with the cane, it's another aspect of the job, correct? They wear suits to work, you carry a cane. I understand that. That's my personal view,' he said, flashing another smile. 'Professionally, however, my duty is to my clients, and what my clients want...well...' He smiled and patted his lap with his long hands. It was impossible for me to think that this man had ever had a mother, that we were the same species.

'For a couple of months now my clients have noticed a certain amount of drop-off from their investments. Key workers are becoming demotivated, uncompetitive, vacating their positions. Aspects of their professions require very specific mindsets and drives, and something is getting in the way of this. To use an old management cliché, it's like some of the cogs are getting sticky, slowing down, and this necessarily affects the whole system.

'Let us be clear on a couple of things. I enjoy clarity in my work, especially when you have clients like mine, where clarity is an alien concept — worse, a dangerous and destructive idea in itself! That's them however, and this is me. You like clarity too I think. Simplicity. Well, I shall try to keep things simple and clear.' He could have been selling me a phone contract, had I not been able to see his black eyes. 'First of all, it is you who has been causing friction, if that's the appropriate phrase, to the system. People come to you, and they lose whatever it is that made them good workers. We've already lost a number, and the ones that don't leave become significantly – in my clients' words, 'drastically' – less profitable. Like any other investment, my clients' money and time has been spent on the assumption that they will be repaid many times over. These people are their investment, are their money. That this margin is being eroded is...irksome.

'Secondly: whatever you have been doing to these people, the effect on the system as a whole is miniscule. To use another analogy, it's not as if you've cut off a whole arm. Rather, one might characterise it as shaving a few cells from the tip of a finger. It's a microscopic effect. Yet, insignificant as it is and you are, my clients are the type that are inclined, once they notice some drag or drain to their resources, no matter how nearly-worthless it is, want it closed off. That's when they call Mr White.'

He sat up and with a swift motion of his hand took the cane from my lap. He turned it in his hands, fitted the pieces together and tapped it on the floor, then he broke it down once more. 'I'm going to look after this for a while, if you don't mind.' I barely nodded, knowing I would never see the cane again. I was lost, I thought, truly lost now. 'It's a miracle we've witnessed today. I say you are not blind, and now you can see!' he said, and laughed. I wish never to hear a laugh like that for as long as I live. 'Well,' he said, standing up 'I'm glad we straightened this all out.' He walked across the lawn, and called over his shoulder, 'See you, then,' and left through the gate and was gone.

For a while I sat on the bench where he left me. It was still early afternoon, and the garden was empty. I stood and as I began to walk, stuck out my arm as if searching in a dark room. I stumbled to the fountain, then sat on the wall and looked down to the floor of it. I could see the coins there at the bottom, each wish becoming rusted over and covered in mould. I walked towards the main gate that led onto a main road, gradually letting my arm drop down, and walking as a sighted person would. I had to learn to make sense of the images around me again, but it was hard. As soon as I left the garden the crush of people landed on me once more, winding me, jostling and shoving for space. I could not see any further ahead than the man in front or beside or behind me. I was invisible again.

Ian Sales has spent the last few years building up a reputation for himself in SF circles, and has recently edited an anthology of his own, called Rocket Science. *I first came across him in an old issue of* Postscripts Magazine, *and I'm delighted to feature one of his stories here.*

Faith

Ian Sales

12 April 1961

At 7,000 metres, a deafening bang fills the capsule, and bright light pours in from above his head. The steel grey of the SIS-1-3KA control panel, with its navigation globe of the earth, glows as if minted in silver. He has only a moment to remark on this before he is catapulted head-first through the hatch. His world, close and spherical and dimly lit, suddenly expands to limitless white. The capsule, a charred and blackened sphere, drops away from him, shrinking as it falls into an ocean of haze. Vostok 1, his *sharik*, his "little ball", he feels deserves a salute for its service, and so he raises a hand in farewell. It kept him free from harm; it protected him from the cold vacuum of space and the fiery inferno of re-entry.

He unbuckles his harness and separates from his ejection seat. For several minutes, they fall together, separated only by a metre or two. Now he feels a deep sadness at being parted from his chair, and reaches out but it is too far away to touch. They have gone where no man has gone before, he and that chair. They have circled the Earth and looked down upon it from a height never before reached. The chair is a part of him: it held him safely, securely, in its embrace; and he rues his need to discard it.

They drift apart as they fall. He rolls over, his back to the chair. The sky in every direction is a blue so pale it is white. There are no clouds and no horizon. He falls through a world of nothing. He cannot see the ground below, he cannot see the sun above him.

His parachute is set to deploy automatically at 2,500 metres. At the speed he is falling, surely he should reach that point soon. He swings out his arms and rolls onto his front. His helmet keeps the rushing air from his face. He has made parachute jumps many times before, but this freefall reminds him of his hour in space. Though he had been strapped into his ejection seat, he had watched in amazement as his hands had drifted of their own accord up before his face. He had felt a lightness in his being, as if he were being called to heaven. 'I feel splendid, very well, very well, very well,' he had told the ground station at Khabarovsk.

Oh, he had felt so very well. Not only privileged, but *chosen*. Closer to God and His dominion. He had experienced such joy, to see the world as God must, to gaze down upon Mother Russia, and the other nations of the world. To know everyone was within his all-encompassing view. A great magnanimity had filled him, made of him a vessel of heavenly light and joy, and he knew the world had changed irrevocably.

Even now, as he falls toward his meeting with the black earth of home, toward his meeting with destiny, he still feels the touch of God. He holds out his arms, as if to embrace the world below him. Yet still he can see nothing, only this limitless haze, this pale white sea of pearlescent light.

It has been more than ten minutes. Why has his chute not deployed? Why has he not reached the ground? Where is his ejection seat?

He falls alone. Forever, he falls.

16 May 1963

The capsule hangs beneath the red-and-white-striped main chute and swings heavily in an abbreviated circle. Within, the astronaut lies on his back, sweating inside his silver pressure suit. The cabin temperature has been rising since the spacecraft suffered a total power failure on the nineteenth orbit. The heat spiked during re-entry, and he thought he might black out. Only the radio and the television camera still function. As he piloted the spacecraft from orbit, he suffered in silence, waving once at the television camera on the instrument panel, just to let them know he was in control, he was *flying* his spacecraft. But now he has deployed the chute, and he lies there and waits, knowing soon that his spacecraft will hit the water at thirty-two feet per second. But he does not know when and he is no longer controlling the spacecraft. Throughout the mission, he has presented his usual laconic self, though it has taken an effort of will to place his safety, his survival, in the hands of pencil necks and rocket scientists.

He keeps his face carefully blank, perhaps just the hint of a smile. He had seen a demonstration of the television before launch, and the picture quality was not very good. He imagines himself a ghost, a blurred figure of white and grey and black seeming to only just inhabit the television screen. The thought prompts another thumbs-up towards the camera.

Though he has remained tensed and expectant for the past ten minutes, splashdown still takes him by surprise. The capsule hits the water, sinks a dozen feet, and then bobs back up sickeningly. Now he is rocking in the swell. He reaches up, unlatches and pulls off his helmet. The interior of the spacecraft is stifling hot, and there is sweat plastered across his brow, but his head still feels a little cooler without the enclosing helmet. He is tempted to blow the hatch, but he remembers only too well what happened to Gus when he did that. He knows some of the others don't like him much, so he has no plans to make himself a target of jokes and sneers by sinking Faith 7.

If he has figured his re-entry correctly, he should be less than ten miles from the USS Kearsage. He can't see anything through the capsule's window but clear blue Pacific sky.

He tells Hawaii he's doing fine, and then radios the aircraft carrier for permission to come aboard. Scott told him this was the correct protocol. They tell him a helicopter is on its way to drop a flotation collar. He wonders if he'll see the aircraft: the window covers only a narrow arc of sky. He should at least hear the whup-whup of its rotor.

He waits patiently. Whenever someone speaks to him on the radio, he replies. But his famous laconism is sorely tested as the minutes stretch by. The capsule is like a bathtub full of boiled air and he wants out. He briefly considers climbing up through the top of the capsule as Scott had done, but elects instead to remain inside.

And then the Kearsage's captain tells him the aircraft carrier is alongside and soon he'll be lifted aboard, but he can see nothing through the window. He has not even seen the Navy frogmen who fitted the flotation collar; assuming the capsule now has such a collar. Surely they would have banged on the hatch to let him know of their arrival? He queries Hawaii, and they confirm the frogmen have done their job.

He feels a sudden and debilitating sense of loneliness, but cannot explain it. The voices on the radio provide some company, but he longs for the sight of a human face. He waves at the television camera, as if the action brings an audience into existence. And so it does, as he's told mission control are waving back at him on the screen they have there.

Now they inform him he's being swung out of the water, but he can still feel the gentle bob and swell of the ocean beneath his back. He can see no ship, no superstructure, no sheer grey wall of ship's hull. Nothing has changed.

Minutes pass. Then a voice on the radio calls his name.

Yeah? he replies.

We just opened the hatch. The capsule is empty.

You got the right spacecraft? he jokes, though he does not find the situation funny.

We can see you on the television, the voice continues. But the capsule is empty.

I'm here, damn it. He holds up a hand to the television camera.

You just put up your hand, yeah we see that. But this capsule, it says Faith 7 on the side but you're not inside. It's empty.

I damn well am inside, he snaps.

But he knows that he sits in a capsule which floats alone in a vast ocean. Were he to blow the hatch, he would be able to see to the horizon in all directions.

And all he would see was water.

3 June 1965

Everyone hears him say, It's the saddest moment of my life; and then they wait for the news that he has re-entered the Gemini 4 spacecraft and the hatch has been latched shut.

The commander leans across to the other seat, ready to help guide his crewmate into his seat and his legs into the footwell. And he waits patiently, hoping he is not going to refuse to come in, as he has been doing for the past ten minutes. He's been out there twenty-three minutes now, the first American to spacewalk. It's going to be hard to get him back in, given he's already complained several times how hot and tired he is.

Then the commander notices that the gold-covered umbilical which snakes out the open hatch has vanished. Puzzled, he sits back in his seat, and then reaches up and struggles to unlatch his hatch. Eventually he manages to open it: it has the same problem with the spring as the other hatch. He undoes his harness and pushes himself up to stand in the open hatchway.

There should be a figure in a white spacesuit floating alongside the capsule.

He can see no one.

There is the Earth beneath him, a curved plain of blue marbled with clouds. Beneath the shifting smears of white, he can see the green and brown of continents rolling past. He twists about but sees only the black heavens and stars, everywhere stars. Keeping firm grip on the lip of the hatch, he leans over the edge of the spacecraft but can see nothing there. If his crewmate had slipped his twenty-three-foot umbilical, he would still be visible. He could not have moved so far away so soon.

His radio is still set on PUSH-TO-TALK, so he cannot speak to Mission Control unless he sits back down in his seat. Reluctantly, he pushes himself back down and fastens his harness. He says, We have a problem. I can't see him.

He's under the spacecraft? asks Capcom. If he is, he needs to get inside right now.

No, he's gone. So has the umbilical.

The radio hisses.

Did you hear me? he asks. I told him to come in, he was coming in, then he just disappeared.

What do you mean, 'disappeared'? He should be tethered.

The umbilical has gone too.

It got loose? The connector disengaged? He has ten minutes of air in a chest-pack.

He's nowhere, the commander insists. One second he was there, the next he'd gone, the umbilical had gone, like they were never there.

Another voice comes on the loop: This is no time for pranks. Is he back in the capsule?

No, he says. I keep on goddamn telling you: he's gone.

And he looks across at the seat beside him and the hatch open above it, the light of Earth shining in, a pearly white light on the empty seat. His crewmate has really gone, he's going to have to pilot this spacecraft back home alone.

He wonders if the Gemini programme can survive this setback. And he wonders at his own callousness in thinking of his crewmate's disappearance as a 'setback'.

It has changed them all, he realises; one man vanishes and the world will never be the same again.

30 June 1971

A pillar of brown dust billows up suddenly into the air as the retros fire, and then the capsule hits the ground with a flat thud. The parachute collapses gracefully to one side and drapes itself across the scrubby grass. For a moment, all is still, a blackened sphere sitting in a circle of black earth. Then the vehicles and helicopters appear. A fleet of trucks and off-road vehicles race across the steppe towards the capsule. They come to a stop some two hundred metres away and people in uniform boil from doors and truckbeds.

Half a dozen technicians, soldiers crowding behind them, gather at the hatch. Quickly, they unscrew the bolts holding the hatch sealed. They are worried: there has been no word from Soyuz 11 since it entered the atmosphere. Even after the ionisation effects had ended and communication was once again possible, the crew did not answer radio calls.

The hatch is lowered carefully to the ground. Everyone pushes forward. They all peer within. The three cosmonauts – Georgiy Timofeyevich Dobrovolsky, Vladislav Nikolayevich Volkov and Viktor Ivanovich Patsayev – are in their seats. They do not look at the open hatch, they do not move. Their faces do not change expression. They should be happy to see the ground crew, they should be smiling at having successfully completed their twenty-two days in orbit aboard Salyut. They have set a world record for the longest time spent in space.

A technician scrambles inside the capsule, though there is very little room. But still he is ignored by the cosmonauts. Dressed in blue coveralls, they remain motionless in their form-fitting seats.

They do not smile, they do not move, they do not breathe. The technician bends over Volkov, and tentatively puts his fingers to the cosmonaut's cheek. His flesh is cold, not with the chill of space but with the chill of a place from which no one ever returns. Both Patsayev and Dobrovolsky are the same. They are, the technician notices, at peace. They have not died violent deaths, but quietly and with deep courage. The technician's heart fills with pride that his country should produce such heroes, that Mother Russia should be made of men such as these.

Later, the technicians and engineers discover what had happened. There is a valve in the hatch which opens to equalise the air pressure inside the capsule as it descends to earth. During

Soyuz 11's separation from Salyut, it had jammed open and all the air inside the capsule had slowly escaped.

But the valve can be closed manually: there is a handle stored beneath one of the seats. This can be attached to the valve. All it needs is nineteen turns.

Nineteen turns.

Pity Patsayev, Dobrovolsky and Volkov. All they had to do was ignore the hiss of air escaping from the spacecraft, ignore the increasing difficulty of breathing, ignore the cold seeping into the capsule, ignore the building pain in their chests, the numbness stealing into their hands and feet...

If only they had the strength to take the handle and attach it to the valve. If only they had the will to make those nineteen turns. And it would be *only* nineteen turns.

Of that, they could be certain.

About the Contributors

Shari Aarlton used to work for the New Zealand government, and likes not doing that any more. Now she leads a rich and satisfying fantasy life instead and says you can't get much better than that.

Justin D. Anderson lives in Morgantown, West Virginia with his wife and son. A former journalist, he's currently finishing an MFA and teaching undergraduate writing at West Virginia University while finalizing the manuscript for a collection of his short stories under the working title *Gardeners*.

His stories have appeared or are forthcoming in *PANK Magazine*, *Cold Mountain Review*, *Controlled Burn*, *Potomac Review*, and elsewhere.

Claire Blechman is from one frozen hinterland or another. She is an honorable-mention-winning writer, thanks in part to her

MFA from Emerson College. Her work has appeared in *Gargoyle*, *Interrobang*, the *Ploughshares* review blog, and the *Vault Guide to the Top 100 Law Firms*. She wrote her whole website by herself, then unimaginatively named it claireblechman.com.

Benjamin Johncock was born in Canterbury, Kent and read Ancient History and Archaeology at the University of Birmingham.

He wanted to be a writer at the age of five and began freelancing when he was a teenager, becoming a regular contributor to a number of national publications, as well as a freelance copywriter and editor.

He is currently working on his first novel, *The Long, Delirious, Burning Blue* and writes for *The Guardian*.

He is 34 and lives in Southwold, Suffolk, with his wife and daughter.

Andrew Jury was born and lives in Leicester, and works part-time for a health and safety company. He's been writing for over twenty years, and had stories appear in *Cemetery Dance*, *Lighthouse 5* and an anthology of speculative fiction, *Dark Doorways*. He also has a story due for publication in a forthcoming issue of *Postscripts*. Andrew's especially influenced by, and in awe of, many post-war US writers, most notably Tobias Wolff, Richard Ford and "the late, great John Cheever".

Harvey Marcus is a freelance writer whose day job is in the marketing department of a commercial publishing house. He has recently completed his first short story collection *How to Fall in Love with an Air Hostess*, of which the title story can be found in our first anthology. He lives in South London with his girlfriend.

Matt Plass lives in Sussex. He works in e-learning, previously edited *Tall Tales & Modern Fables* magazine and is one half of Bread and Love Productions.

Ian Sales wanted to be an astronaut when he grew up but sadly wasn't born in the USA or USSR. So now he writes stories about them. He has been published in *Jupiter*, *Postscripts*, *Alt Hist*, and the anthologies *Catastrophia*, *Vivisepulture* and *The Monster Book for Girls*. He has recently published an anthology of hard sf, *Rocket Science*, for Mutation Press, along with a hard sf novella, *Adrift on the Sea of Rains*. He reviews books for *Interzone*, and is represented by the John Jarrold Literary Agency.

Mandy Taggart lives with her family on the North Coast of Ireland. Her short fiction has appeared in various publications including Cobalt Review, Specter, and WordPlaySound audio magazine. She was a finalist for the 5th Micro Award, and a top contender for the Glass Woman ghost story prize in 2011.

For more information on the contributors
to this volume, please visit our website:

www.thefictiondesk.com/authors

Also from The Fiction Desk:

Various Authors
the first Fiction Desk anthology

These stories will take you from the shores of Lake Garda in Italy to a hospital room in Utah, from a retirement home overlooking the Solent to an unusual school in the wilds of Scotland. Meet people like Daniel, a government employee looking for an escape; and William, a most remarkable dog by anyone's standards.

Various Authors is the first volume in our new series of anthologies dedicated to discovering and publishing the best new short fiction.

New stories by:

Charles Lambert	Matthew Licht
Lynsey May	Ben Lyle
Jon Wallace	Danny Rhodes
Patrick Whittaker	Harvey Marcus
Adrian Stumpp	Alex Cameron
Jason Atkinson	Ben Cheetham

Avilable to order from all good British bookshops,
or online at www.thefictiondesk.com.

£9.99
Out now.
ISBN 9780956784308

Also from The Fiction Desk:

All These Little Worlds

the second Fiction Desk anthology

Among the stories in our second anthology: a new dress code causes havoc in an American school, a newspaper mistake leads a retired comedian to look back over a not-quite-spotless career, and a family buys an unusual addition to their fish tank.

This volume also features 'Pretty Vacant', a special long story from Charles Lambert.

New stories by:

Charles Lambert	Colin Corrigan
Jason Atkinson	Ryan Shoemaker
Halimah Marcus	Jennifer Moore
Andrew Jury	Mischa Hiller
James Benmore	

Avilable to order from all good British bookshops,
or online at www.thefictiondesk.com.

£9.99
Out now.
ISBN 9780956784322

Subscribe
one year - four volumes
for just
£36.95
(wherever you are in the world).

Subscribing to our anthology series is the best way to support out publishing programme and keep yourself supplied with the best new short fiction from the UK and abroad. It costs just £36.95 for a year (four volumes).

We publish a new volume roughly every three months. Each one has its own title: *The Maginot Line* is volume three. The next volume is due in late summer 2012.

Subscribe online:
www.thefictiondesk.com/subscribe

(Price correct at time of going to press, but may change over time; please see website for current pricing.)